D1186669

A Scottish Feast is an anthology of the best of writing by Scots on the subject of food, appetite and eating. Librarian and author Hamish Whyte and food writer Catherine Brown have collected over one hundred extracts—poems, fiction, non-fiction and letters, not forgetting the occasional recipe.

Dunbar's account of Edinburgh as a gastronomic heaven; Dr Johnson scoffing Scotch Broth; Para Handy and the recipe for chuckie soup; James Kelman on mince and tatties; Edwin Morgan's strawberry feast—from these and many more, perhaps we may truly judge a nation from what enters its stomach!

A Scottish Feast is a feast of writing.

A Scottish Feast

an anthology of food and eating

Edited by
Hamish Whyte and Catherine Brown

First published 1996
Argyll Publishing
Glendaruel
Argyll PA22 3AE
Scotland

**British Library Cataloguing-in-Publication Data.
A catalogue record for this book is available
from the British Library.**

ISBN 1 874640 42 4

Origination
Cordfall Ltd, Glasgow

Printing
Bookcraft (Bath) Ltd

To Mary Baxter MBE
for her long service to PEN, Scottish writers
and the culinary arts

contents

acknowledgements

We would like to thank the many people who made this book possible: the contributors who freely allowed their work to be used, all those who suggested possible items for inclusion (sorry we couldn't use them all) and publishers who generously waived reprint fees:

Hayley Berry and Anthony Sheil and Associates, Simon Berry (whose idea *A Feast* was), Valerie Bierman, Sheena Blackhall, Alan Bold, Curtis Brown Associates, George Mackay Brown, Margaret Gillies Brown, George Bruce, Moira Burgess, Elizabeth Burns, Larry Butler, Thorbjörn Campbell and the Saltire Society, John Carswell, Elizabeth Casciani, James Clark and Canongate Books, Derek Cooper, Robert Crawford, Alan Davidson & A.P. Watt Ltd, Douglas Dunn, Faber and Faber, John Farquharson Ltd, Ian Hamilton Finlay, David Fletcher Associates, Graham Fulton, Robin Fulton, Janice Galloway, Duncan Glen, Aladair Gray, Cliff Hanley, L. Healey and Bloodaxe Books, Mairi Hedderwick, Archie Hind, Tom Hubbard, Willie Hunter, Alexander Hutchison, Rosemary Innes, Tom Johnstone and Mercat Press, Jackie Kay, James Kelman, A.L. Kennedy, Alison Kermack, David Kinloch, Alanna Knight, Robbie Kydd, Kylin Press, Tom Leonard, Maurice Lindsay, Robin Lloyd-Jones, Liz Lochhead, Brian McCabe, Mary McCann, Carl MacDougall, Janette McGinn, Catherine McInerney and the Association for Scottish Literary Studies, Rosemary Mackay, Peter Mackenzie and Mainstream Publishing, Duncan McLean, Adam McNaughtan, Naomi Mitchison, Edwin Moore, Edwin Morgan, Ken Morrice, David Morrison, Isobel Murray, Thom Nairn, Donny O'Rourke, Janet Paisley, Reed Books, Dilys Rose, Michael Schmidt and Carcanet Press, Cath Scott, Jeanie Scott and Polygon, Paul Scott, Scottish National Dictionary Association Ltd, Christopher Small, Iain Crichton Smith, Robin Smith and the Trustees of the National Library of Scotland, Muriel Spark, Elizabeth Sutherland, Emma Tennant, Derick Thomson, Geddes Thomson, Valerie Thornton,

James A. Troup and the Orkney Natural History Society,
Gael and Jill Turnbull, Vintage Press (for 'The Appetite' from
Intimate Voices© Tom Leonard), Virago Press, Howard Watson
and Random House, Irvine Welsh, Brian Whittingham,
Winifred Whyte, Gordon Wright.

And special thanks go to Colleen Godley and Laura Fiorentini of Scottish
PEN for their assistance.
We apologise to anyone omitted from the above. Every effort was
made to trace copyright holders. The editors and publisher would be
pleased to be notified of any corrections.

introduction

Something as basic as food has always played an important part in literature. The most famous example is probably Proust's tea-soaked madeleine. Another random example is Steinbeck's short story *Breakfast* in which you can almost smell the bacon frying and bread baking and share the comradeship of the dusty road. Food in literature is a huge subject and still relatively unexplored; in Scottish literature even more so. Regard the bleeding chunks in this collection (the term 'pieces' is appropriate) merely as starters for a much wider menu.

Is it possible to detect a national obsession with food? 'Food as Metaphor in Scottish Fiction' just could be a thesis topic. How many scenes of family strife (and reconciliation) have we encountered round a table (see Carswell, Gray, Welsh), how many scenes of seduction enhanced by sensual eating (cf. Morgan, Fulton, Leonard, McCann)? Can you eat a Scotch pie again without thinking of Rosemary Mackay's schoolgirl salival lunchtime ecstasy? No doubt we all have our own madeleines, whether pineapple cubes with cream, strawberries and sugar, skirlie and mince or Scotch pies eaten with tomatoes and HP sauce (on the rocks at Troon).

Some writers don't have much time for food in their work—Norman MacCaig for one (drink was another matter!)—while in Edwin Morgan's world his characters are always hungering for something. You can't avoid food in Janice Galloway's fiction, disgusting, delicious, deplorable or desirable (see especially 'The Meat', 'Two Fragments' and *The Trick is to Keep Breathing, passim*).

But, of course, the Scot who has had arguably the greatest influence on the national identity in food is Burns.

> Fair fa' your honest, sonsie face,
> Great Chieftan o' the Puddin-race!
> Aboon them a' ye tak your place,
> Painch, tripe, or thairm:
> Weel are ye wordy of a grace
> As lang's my arm.

First and foremost 'To a Haggis' strikes the celebratory note, dear to Scottish hearts, while at the same time honouring something which has little, if any, visual appeal. It was entirely appropriate that Burns should celebrate a haggis. Do not judge by appearances, he says. Honour the honest virtues of sense and worth, not in French ragouts and fricassees, but in a dish which takes the parts of an animal—that some would throw to the dogs—and makes something worth celebrating.

It was a challenge, firstly to Scots. But as it has turned out, also to the rest of the world, as the Burns Supper celebration of sense and worth has taken on a universal meaning. Yet at the same time it leaves the Scots with a very strong national food image: 'an assertion', says James Kinsley, 'of peasant virtue and strength, expressed in harsh violent diction and images of slaughter.' There is no escape from reality in Burns's poem, or from the picture of Scottish food as hearty, wholesome, unsophisticated, distinctive, warming and comforting.

Historically, the Scots come into the category of poor Northern Europeans, used to scrimping and saving; thrifty, yet able to make good-tasting and warming food out of scant resources: broths, stovies, skirlie, clapshot, dumplings and puddings, to name but a few. When this is combined with a strong sense of national celebration and feasting, in hospitable and open-hearted ways, it becomes unique. Burns captures it all in 'To a Haggis'.

This anthology was originally going to be divided by subject— 'Breakfasts', 'Feasts', 'Romance and the Scottish Palate' and so on, but in the end it was thought simpler to arrange the material alphabetically by author and allow the readers to make their own connections and contrasts. The extracts are taken mainly from poetry and fiction, but some nonfiction, recipes and short pieces have been scattered throughout for added flavour.

The impetus behind *A Scottish Feast* was to raise funds for the Scottish branch of PEN, the international writers organisation, in the run-up to the International Congress of PEN in Edinburgh in 1997. Suggestions were canvassed from members and other writers and the editors' own larders were raided. The collection is therefore of necessity selective, but we hope it serves as a stimulus to sample the wealth of Scots cuisine, and of course Scottish literature, and as a welcome to all visitors.

Hamish Whyte, Catherine Brown, February 1996

'To a Haggis' Robert Bryden (1865-1940s)
from *A Series of Burns Etchings* (1896)
(courtesy The Mitchell Library, Glasgow City Libraries)

Mince and Tatties

I dinna like hail tatties
Pit on my plate o mince
For when I tak my denner
I eat them baith at yince.

Sae mash and mix the tatties
Wi mince intil the mashin,
And sic a tasty denner
Will aye be voted "Smashin!"

J.K. Annand (1908-93)
A Wale O' Rhymes, Edinburgh: Macdonald (1989)

Aiberdonian Recipe

Takk seeds o Nor East stock (twa)
Plunk them thegither
Simmer fur awhile.
Dinna byle (it tends tae spyle the flavour)
Add ae spirk o ile
A shakk o satty sea
A suppie cauld snaw bree
A guid Scots tongue tae gie it virr an birr
A toosht o barley
Fang o granite chukkies
A Finnan haddie
Fur nine month, let it staun . . .
Syne, wheek it up,
Skelp its dock
Rowe't in a cloot
Cowp it frae the pan
An there ye'll hae't
A fire-new Aiberdonian!

Sheena Blackhall (b. 1947)

Sheep's Head

Before Dr Johnson came to breakfast, Lady Lochbuy said, "he was a *dungeon* of wit"; a very common phrase in Scotland to express a profoundness of intellect, though he afterwards told me that he never had heard it. She proposed that he should have some cold sheep's-head for breakfast. Sir Allan seemed displeased at his sister's vulgarity, and wondered how such a thought should come into her head. From a mischievous love of sport, I took the lady's part; and very gravely said, "I think it but fair to give him an offer of it. If he does not choose it, he may let it alone." "I think so," said the lady, looking at her brother with an air of victory. Sir Allan, finding the matter desperate, strutted about the room, and took snuff. When Dr Johnson came in, she called to him, "Do you choose any cold sheep's-head, sir?" "No, madam," said he, supposing he had refused it to save the trouble of bringing it in. They thus went on at cross-purposes, till he confirmed his refusal in a manner not to be misunderstood; while I sat quietly by, and enjoyed my success.

James Boswell (1740-95)
Journal of a Tour to the Hebrides (1785)

Scotch Broth

At dinner, Dr Johnson ate several plate-fulls of Scotch broth, with barley and peas in it, and seemed very fond of the dish. I said, "You never ate it before."—"No, sir; but I don't care how soon I eat it again."

19

A Real Steak Pie?

In a long life of dining out the late Jack House used a steak pie as his test of a good restaurant. "Can they make a real steak pie?" he would enquire when you recommended a new restaurant to him. "If it turns out to be a sort of casserole steak with a square of pastry on top, then watch out!"

The love of his life was Glasgow, where he worked as a journalist and author, and for a time wrote an Eating Out column in the *Scottish Field*, though he claimed no association with professional gourmets. To his mind they were a suspect race who chattered too self-indulgently for his liking.

There were no flights of fancy in his column, no pretentious gastronomic pronouncements. He dealt with the facts, the good, the bad, the old, the new, the gossip, the comfort, the service, or the lack of it. He was happy that people called him a bon viveur, and often laughed about 'living the life of Riley', but his favourite description of himself was an aristologist.

"What, you don't know what an aristologist is? According to my dictionary, aristology is the art of dining."

In Jack's post-World War II eating-out heyday, sophisticated Glasgow restaurants included the Mal Maison, the One-o-One and Ferrari's, but he thought that the best steak pie was at the Boulevard Hotel in unfashionable Clydebank and he went back so many times—as he did to many other restaurants which passed his test—that they kept a table which became known as 'Mr House's Table'.

Straightforward reporting was his discipline, but he drew the line at writing recipes. "I can hardly boil an egg," he would say. "How can you expect me to write a recipe." So we will never know more of the steak pie at the Boulevard Hotel, except that to pass the House Test it must have been properly made, no unattached lids, no skimping on good ingredients.

Steak Pie

INGREDIENTS for 4-5:
2 tablespoons beef dripping, or oil
1 large onion, finely chopped
1 1b (500g) rump steak
6-8 oz (200-250 g) ox kidney or beef sausages
1 tablespoon plain flour, seasoned with salt and pepper
water or stock
half a teaspoon ground cloves
1 tablespoon parsley, chopped
1 tablespoon marjoram, chopped
8 oz (250 g) medium-sized mushrooms (optional)
2 pint (1 litre) pie-dish and pie funnel or cup
6 oz (200 g) puff pastry
Beaten egg for brushing

METHOD Making the filling: Heat the oil and brown the onions until dark, but not burnt. Brown the sausages. Skin, split, core and cut up kidney. Using a rolling-pin, or meat-bat, beat out the rump steak until thin. Cut into long strips. Coat the meat with seasoned flour. Cut sausages in half. Roll meat around either the sausages or the kidney. Put into the base of the pie-dish, end on. Add seasonings. Cover with onions. Pile whole mushrooms on top, so that they come up high above the rim. They will hold up the pastry so a pie funnel will not be necessary. Pour over enough water to come three-quarters of the way up the filling.

Baking the pie: Pre-heat the oven to 450F/230C Gas 8. Roll out the pastry an inch or so larger than the pie, cut round pie to fit. Wet rim of pie-dish. Cut a thin strip from the leftover pastry and place round rim, wet edge, and place on pastry lid. Seal down well. Use leftover pastry for pastry leaves. Brush top and leaves with beaten egg, place on leaves, make two holes for steam to escape. Bake for about 30 minutes in the hot oven until the pastry is risen and browned. Reduce the heat to 350F/180C gas 4 and bake for another hour until the meat is cooked. If the pastry is browning too much, cover with foil. Fill up the pie with hot water or stock before serving.

Catherine Brown *The Herald*, December 1991

Butter

What's come of my churning? The van-man, he took seven pounds, and a basket of warm eggs, for jam, sugar, tea, paraffin. I gave the tinkers a lump, to keep the black word from our byre. I put some on the damp peats, to coax a flame. I swear the cat has a yellow tongue. There was only a scrape for the fisherman's bannock, like a bit of sun on a dull day. The old cow is giving me a mad look.

George Mackay Brown (b. 1921)
Fishermen with Ploughs, Hogarth Press (1971)

Clapshot

The other day, by way of a treat, I brought a piece of steak for grilling. Would clapshot go with grilled steak? No harm in trying. I peeled carefully the precious 'golden wonders'—and thought what a shame, in a way, 'golden wonders' being so delicious boiled in their thick dark jackets. And while the tatties and neeps where ramping away on the top of the electric grill, it came into my mind that somewhere, a while back, I had read a recipe for clapshot that advised an onion to be added. (It may be in one of the books of F Marian McNeill, the Orkney-born connoisseur of food and ancient Scottish lore.)

In no time at all I had an onion stripped and chopped and delivered (my eyes weeping) among the neeps and tatties in the rampaging pot. . . . Fifteen minutes later the probing fork told me that all was ready. Decant the water into the sink, set the pot on the kitchen floor on top of last week's *Radio Times*, add a golden chunk of butter and a dash of milk, then salt and plenty of pepper, and begin to mash. . . .

Everything about clapshot is good, including the smell and colour. I think this particular clapshot, with the onion in it, was about the best I've ever made. And it blended magnificently on the palate with the grilled steak. And it made a glow in the wintry stomach.

Everything good about clapshot? I have a certain reservation about the name. It sounds more like some kind of missile used in the Thirty Years' War than the name of a toothsome dish and yet I've no doubt the roots of the word are ancient, worthy, and venerable. As soon as I've finished writing this I must dip into *The Orkney Norn*.

George Mackay Brown
Under Brinkie's Brae, Edinburgh: Gordon Wright (1979)

The Meal

She likes to have a hand in happiness
and knowing we had visitors
gave a fillet of smoked salmon
from wild fish of northern waters.
The deep pink succulence
lay on white porcelain
encircled by dark rimmed wheels
of pale green cucumber —
On top a wedge or two of lemon:
Nearby, a mound of crusty bread,
brown and buttered,
A wooden mill holding black peppercorns.

Afterwards beef
bred in lush green fields
then iced-creams from Galloway
with tang of whisky, honey, strawberry.

Sitting on chairs around the table
the talk was of the place we'd visited —
The House of Dun —
An Adam house of Erskine heritage
and how, on this rainy afternoon,
two hours had flown
enjoying its story and its treasures —
Millicent's generosity,
Augusta's needlework,
Violet Jacob's poetry —
And vistas from wide windows
of fields, woods, water.

The drink was Elderflower
The wine —

A happy glow of Bramble.

Margaret Gillies Brown (previously unpublished)

To Cook a Kipper

Only the aged are likely to have enjoyed the true succulence and taste of the kippered herring. Since I am one of these it behoves me to divulge the procedures which will restore these culinary delights to others. So remarkable were they to me in my childhood in the early twenties, that near twenty years later I referred to the experience of the cooking of the kipper as the climax of my poem, *The Curtain*.

One stormy night in the port of Fraserburgh, my home-town, I had been left in the charge of an old woman who was telling me a fearful tale until it was interrupted by the return of my parents. The following night the storm had gone, but a thick mist enveloped the town. It was time for bed, but I was afraid to go upstairs, past the tall curtain which concealed an alcove, for the solution to the 'unfinished tale' would be revealed, and it involved my death. A noise at the front door put an end to my prevarications to my mother. We rushed to it and there was my father:

> My father came home,
> His clothes sea-wet,
> His breath cold.
> He said a boat had gone.

My fears vanished; my mind sought for comfortable images. The poem ends:

> I smelt again
> The kippers cooked in oak-ash.
> That helped me to forget
> The tall curtain.

For such kippers there was no veneer of the brown dye, which gives the impression of herring long hung in smoke, though the deception is immediately evident as a greasy brown liquid slips from the fish as it cooks in the pan. But herewith the whole requirement:

Fresh herring
Hang on rack in a kiln for twelve hours.
Smoke from oak chips in small heaps
                              on the floor of the kiln.
Immediately at the end of the process
wrap herring individually in grease-proof paper,
and thrust into the ash embers of the chips
for approximately three minutes.
Eat with fingers.

Today some kippers are not dyed, in which case the first procedure may be dispensed with.

George Bruce (b. 1909)
(written for this book)

Of all the fish that swim in the sea
The herring is the fish for me

Scottish Folk Song

The Laird's Wife
Visits the Poorhouse

she brings me roses
pink and fullblown ones
tight-budded white ones
does she think I can eat
these sweet petals?
will the sight of them
fill my stomach?
what colour are a bunch of flowers
in this peat-smoked
one-candled cupboard
of a room?
can their scent
drown out its stench?
roses
and here each inch
of land taken up with
potatoes   turnip   barley
a rose bush?
it would be pulled up
by its thorny branches
the earth dug greedily
planted with food
and she —
and she —
her ladyship —
I will strip the petals
from these flowers
with my teeth
chew them up
spit the bitter pulp
and woody stems
onto the fire

burn them as fuel
that they might have some use
and may their smoke
choke her as she walks away
may the perfume of her garden
that she tells us is so famous
turn sour as burning flesh
and may her pink and white skin
be stripped from her bones
and spat to herring gulls

I bury my face
in bitter roses
and begin to bite

Elizabeth Burns
New Writing Scotland 7, ASLS (1989)

As soon as the collops were ready, Cluny gave them, with his own hand, a squeeze of lemon. . . . They are such as I gave His Royal Highness (Prince Charles Edward Stuart) in this very house.

Robert Louis Stevenson
Kidnapped (1886)

To a Haggis

Fair fa' your honest, sonsie face,
Great Chieftan o' the Puddin-race!
Aboon them a' ye tak your place,
                Painch, tripe, or thairm:
Weel are ye wordy of a *grace*
                As lang's my arm.

The groaning trencher there ye fill,
Your hurdies like a distant hill,
Your *pin* wad help to mend a mill
                In time o' need,
While thro' your pores the dews distil
                Like amber bead.

His knife see Rustic-labour dight,
An' cut you up wi' ready slight,
Trenching your gushing entrails bright
                Like onie ditch;
And then, O what a glorious sight,
                Warm-reekin, rich!

Then, horn for horn they stretch an' strive,
Deil tak the hindmost, on they drive,
Till a' their weel-swall'd kytes belyve
                Are bent like drums;
Then auld Guidman, maist like to rive,
                Bethankit hums.

Is there that owre his French *ragout*,
Or *olio* that wad staw a sow,
Or *fricassee* wad make her spew
                Wi' perfect sconner,
Looks down wi' sneering, scornfu' view
                On sic a dinner?

Poor devil! see him owre his trash,
As feckless as a wither'd rash,
His spindle shank a guid whip-lash,
                    His nieve a nit;
Thro' bluidy floor or field to dash,
                    O how unfit!

But mark the Rustic, *haggis-fed*,
The trembling earth resounds his tread,
Clap in his walie nieve a blade,
                    He'll mak it whissle;
An' legs, an' arms, an' heads will sned,
                    Like taps o' thrissle.

Ye Pow'rs wha mak mankind your care,
And dish them out their bill o' fare,
Auld Scotland wants nae skinking ware
                    That jaups in luggies;
But, if ye wish her gratefu' pray'r,
                    Gie her a *Haggis*!

Robert Burns (1759-96)
Poems, Kilmarnock (1786)

Faulkner said
the only thing
worth writing about
is the conflict
in the heart

I think vegetable
I speak vegetable

I eat vegetable
I am vegetable

I am vegetable

But nestled
in the heart
of my first lettuce
freshly delivered
from Ayrshire Organics –

A tiny black slug
I almost ate it

How many others
did I eat?

I am slug
I am slug

Larry Butler (1995)
(previously unpublished)

Catherine Carswell

Taking Lunch
the Edinburgh Way

And now Aunt Georgina had helped them all to soup from a silver tureen. Georgie was sipping hers in what she knew to be the correct way, from the side of the spoon instead of from the tip as she did at home; and Joanna had nervously raised a glass of water to her lips, when she caught her aunt's eye upon her.

"We don't usually drink water before our soup, Joanna," said Mrs Balmain quietly. "At least," she added, "I don't know how you do in Glasgow. In Edinburgh it is thought vulgar to drink immediately before food. Besides it is bad for the stomach."

Joanna crimsoned and put down her glass untouched. Neither her mother's kind, grieved glance nor the message of sympathy sent across the table from Georgie's eyes could salve her wound. Though a murderous hatred of her aunt rose in her, she unhesitatingly condemned herself. She had not known any better than to drink water before food, and now she sat disgraced before them all—particularly before Cousin Irene, for whom that very morning at breakfast she had conceived a violent admiration. Oh! why were she and her family not in keeping with the elegance around them.

Catherine Carswell (1879-1946)
Open The Door Andrew Melrose (1920)

The Plaza

Also in Edinburgh, in September 1926, the Plaza Salon de Danse and cafe opened its doors.

Like all other ballrooms, the Plaza was not licensed for alcohol but patrons had a choice of tea, coffee, Horlicks, cold milk, hot milk or Bovril. High teas cost one and ninepence and wedding guests were catered for at four and sixpence per head. The 'usual wedding menu' for four and sixpence was: tea, coffee, various sandwiches, sandwich fingers, muffins, cakes, cut cake, shortbreads, assorted pastries, biscuits and chocolate biscuits, fruit and wine jellies and creams, trifle, fruit salad, ices handed round later and 'aerated waters' (lemonades).

For grander affairs there was the five and sixpence menu: Soup or grapefruit, choice of hot joints or beefsteak pies with vegetables and potatoes, cold meats and salad, choice of two sweets, tea, coffee, biscuits and cheese, sandwiches, cakes, biscuits and ices served later.

Elizabeth Casciani
Oh, how we danced, Edinburgh: Mercat Press (1994)

The drop biscuits and almond biscuits that so often appeared heaped high between dishes of jelly, cream and syllabub on the dinner-table, at dessert, might also be offered at tea.

Marion Lochhead
The Scots Household in the Eighteenth Century Moray Press (1948)

A Bit Denner

Miss Menie Trotter, of the Mortonhall family, was of a later date. She was of the agrestic order. Her pleasure lay in the fields and long country walks. Ten miles at a stretch, within a few years of her death, was nothing to her. Her attire accorded. But her understanding was fully as masculine. Though slenderly endowed, she did, unnoticed, acts of liberality for which most of the rich would expect to be advertised. Prevailing loneliness gave her some entertaining habits, but never impaired her enjoyment of her friends, for whom she had always diverting talk, and occasionally "a bit denner". Indeed she generally sacrificed an ox to hospitality every autumn, which, according to a system of her own, she ate regularly from nose to tail; and as she indulged in him only on Sundays, and with a chosen few, he feasted her half through the winter. This was at Blackford Cottage, a melancholy villa on the north side of Blackford Hill, where the last half, at the least, of her life was passed. I remember her urging her neighbour Sir Thomas Lauder, not long before her death, to dine with her next Sunday—"For, eh! Sir Thammas! we're terrible near the tail noo."

Henry Cockburn (1779-1854)
Memorials of his Time (1856)

O, the West Coast Breakfast

O, those west coast breakfasts! Remember descending into the saloon of the M.V. *Lochnevis* on her morning run south from Portree in the thirties? Tea the colour of mahogany handrails, pink fleshy Mallaig kippers, eggs laid by hens joyously unconfined, rounds of Ayrshire bacon.

Remember even further back to breakfasts on the *Iona* sailing down the Clyde from Greenock in the 1870s. "Oh, that breakfast," wrote a voyager, "never did I part with a florin with greater pleasure. Cutlets of salmon fresh from the water, sausages of great tenderness and delicacy. Coffee hot and aromatic and suggestive of Araby the blest; marmalade of all kinds, with bread-and-butter and toast all equally good."

And then those even more substantial breakfasts laid for early travellers. The smoked beef, cheese, fresh eggs, salted herrings, butter milk and cream, blaeberry jam, tea, coffee and Jamaica rum provided for the Frenchman Faujas St Fond at Torloisk on Mull in 1784 and the early morning banquet presented to John Knox two years later in the Hebrides: "a dram of whisky, gin, rum or brandy, plain or infused with berries that grow among the heath, French rolls, oat and barley bread, tea and coffee, honey in the comb, red and blackcurrant jellies, marmalade, conserves and excellent cream, fine-flavoured butter, fresh and salted; Cheshire and Highland cheese, a plateful of very fresh eggs, fresh and salted herrings, ditto haddocks and whitings, cold round of venison, beef and mutton hams. . ."

Last summer, cromak in hand I took the road to the isles by Tummel and Loch Rannoch and Lochaber looking for the perfect west coast breakfast and what food I found!

Plates of porridge so thick and salty and substantial you could cut yourself slices with a knife; bowls of cream to dip your spoon into and bread hot from the oven. O, the finnan haddie at Glenfinnan, the buttered eggs at Achiltibuie, the Loch Fyne golden kippers at Inverary, the crisp bacon and fried eggs in every but and ben. O, the Loch Morar marmalade, the heather honey of Eriskay, the breakfast baps at Brodick, the scalding pots of Taynuilt tea, the butter yellow scrambled eggs of Scarinish, the bannocks of Arisaig plucked from the girdle, the preserves of Plockton, the hot scones of Scalpay. Food to dream and drool about!

And dreaming I awoke.

"Fruit juice or flakes?" asked the New Zealand lassie in her MacMarks tartan kilt.

On the table lay an assemblage of convenience goodies. Mini-pots of lime marmalade, domino-sized foil-pax of Kerrygold butter, terribly refined sachets of Tate & Lyle sugar.

The porridge when it came was a runny poultice tasting of cardboard made by stirring water unenthusiastically into a packet mix. To my Oat-Brek ("Wrap your kiddies in winter warmth and grain-fresh goodness") I added a few drops of UHT milk or was it powdered Skimmo?

The tea-bag tea was thin, the toasted Grannie's Pride bread was limp as a loofah. I spread it with butter from my little doll's house tub and tackled my boiled egg which tasted egregiously of fishmeal. Supposing Dr Johnson had been confronted with this rubbish; would he have swept it impetuously from the table?

What was it he said? – "He who does not mind his belly will hardly mind anything else."

When Johnson made his jaunt to the western isles they gave him barley bannocks, coffee and tea in genteel order, marmalade of oranges, cream and brose, abundance of fish, the marks of a good table.

Not rice crispies and reconstituted orange juice!

Come back west coast breakfast. Come back sugar in generous if unhygienic bowls and big pats of butter on openhearted plates. Come back creamy milk in jugs, porridge made with roughground oats, fish from the seas, bread looking like bread and not like anaemic slices of surgical lint.

And come back soon.

Derek Cooper (1979)

Miss Cranston's Tea Menu

Tea Room Prices

Plain Tea, Coffee, Cocoa, Small Cup	2 1/2d
" " " Large Cup	3 1/2d
Chocolate per Small Cup	3 1/2d
Extra Hot Water (per person)	1d
Clear Soup	3d
Aerated Waters, Large	3d
Small Hot or Cold Milk	2 1/2d
Small Glass Buttermilk	1d
Bread or Scone and Butter	1 1/2d
Cakes, French or Plain	1 1/2d
Hot Toasted Scone and Butter	2d
Slice of Toast	2d
Cheddar or Dunlop Cheese	3d
Jam or Marmalade	1 1/2d
Ham Sandwiches	2d & 4d
Hot Mutton Pie	4d
Scrambled or Poached Eggs on Toast	8d
Small " " "	5d
Scrambled Egg and Cheese	7d
Weish Rarebit	5d
Buck "	8d

SNACK TEAS from 3 till 7.30.

Fried Split Haddock	11d
" Whiting	10d
Small Fish Cake	5d
Kippered Herring	5d
Small Potted do.	3 1/2d
Ham & Egg	8d
Sausages & Bacon	8d
Boiled Country Egg	4d
Hot Mutton Pie	4d
Small Cold Veal Pie & Salad	4d
Potted Meat & do.	4 1/2d
Cold Roast Beef & do.	10d
Honey Vanilla Ice	5d

HIGH TEAS from 3 till 7. 30

FIXED PRICE HIGH TEAS.

	Ham and Egg or	
PRICE	Filleted Fish	
1/3	3 Breads Varied	
	Pot of Tea	
	Ham and Eggs or	
PRICE	Filleted Fish & Chips	
1/6	3 Breads Varied	
	Pot of Tea	

A LA CARTE
HIGH TEAS

Cold Tay Salmon & Salad	1/1
Mayonnaise of Salmon & Salad	1/1
Fried Cod Steak	11d
Aberdeen Haddock	11d
Fried Haddock	11d
" Whiting	10d
Baked Fish Custard	9d
Kippered Herring	5d
Potted do.	5d
Fried Bacon & Eggs	8d & 1/-
" " & Sausages	1/-
" Sausages & Eggs	1/-
Wiltshire Bacon & Poached Eggs	1/-
Chicken & Ham Rissole & Sauce	9d
Fried Turkey Egg	6d
Small Cold Roast Lamb	10d
" " Beef	10d
" " Tongue	10d
" " Do & Ham	10d
" " Round of Beef	10d
Cup of Tea (small)	2 1/2d
" " " (large)	3 1/2d
Pot of Teas (Newly infused)	
per person	4d
Slice of Toast	2d
Butter Bread or Scone	1 1/2d
Cakes Various	1 1/2d
Preserves	1 1/2d

Kate Cranston operated tearooms in Glasgow at the turn of the nineteeenth century, empoying E. A. Walton and C. R. Mackintosh to design them.

Scotch Broth

A soup so thick you could shake its hand
And stroll with it before dinner.

The face rising to its surface,
A rayfish waiting to stroked,

Is the pustular, eat-me face of a crofter,
Turnipocephalic, white-haired.

Accepting all comers, it's still our nation's
Flagsoup, sip-soup; sip, sip, sip

At this other scotch made with mutton
That intoxicates only

With peas and potatoes, chewy uists of meat.
All races breath over our bowl,

Inhaling Inverness and Rutherglen,
Waiting for a big teuchtery face

To compose itself from carrots and barley
Rising up towards the spoon

Robert Crawford (b. 1959)
Masculinity, Cape (1996)

A Kipper With My Tea

My boyhood holidays were almost all spent with my grandparents in Bearsden, a fearsome-sounding but placid suburb of Glasgow. I will not attempt to explain why he was called Twinko and she Merdy, but there were reasons which seem valid to the family.

Merdy rose at six, and I not much later, for the treats of the day began early. First, I was allowed to ride with the milkman in his great big, battered, open-top Humber, as he delivered the milk to the other houses in South Erskine Park. Then, having run triumphantly back down the road, I could repeat the experience with the butcher's van, a less splendid vehicle and a slower progression, for the butcher's business required more discussion. And then it would be time for breakfast.

It was many years later, long after my grandparents were dead, that I was told about Merdy's secret relationship with this butcher. When he brought her meat from the van he would whisper the name of a horse he fancied in a race that afternoon, and Merdy would give him sixpence, or even a shilling, to wager on it. Sometimes he would bring many shillings back and slip them to her. The entire operation was financed by a minuscule margin in Merdy's modest housekeeping allowance, and Twinko knew nothing of it.

This apart, Merdy was transparent, a true innocent whose pleasure it was to count her blessings (Twinko being number one), feed her hens, pick her roses, spoil—but only to a measured extent—her grandson, and exercise her skill in the kitchen.

Culinary literature abounds with references to people who declare that this or that—an apple pie, perhaps—was only really right when made by 'grandmother'; and there is frequently an implication that memory is playing tricks. I haven't myself often come across people saying such things, but I have no hesitation in saying that there were certain things which Merdy made uniquely well, and am fortified in this belief by the fact that everyone agreed at the time—it is not a case of my memory being faulty or correct but a phenomenon which was apparent to all there and then.

We still have her baking tins, and my wife is convinced that they work better than anything of modern making—but not the way they worked for Merdy. My own mother, a good cook herself, would work beside Merdy in the kitchen, trying to duplicate precisely everything she did, and would of course produce excellent scones or whatever as a result, but scones which still lacked that Merdy-cachet. A puzzle.

Anyway, the evening routine at South Erskine Park was that Twinko, a timber merchant, would return from the city soon after five, and very soon after that we would all sit down on high-backed mohair chairs round the dining table and have a really lavish high tea. The savoury dish might be fish custard, or mince, or any of many other things—but every now and then it would be kippers. After this, and the accompanying bread and butter, would come the procession of scones, pancakes, biscuits, cakes (small) and cakes (large). For each item there was an appropriate plate, and I still have three of them, one oblong, one oval and one round. The round one was for a cake (large) which might be a Black Bun, a really rich confection which would always be eaten last.

Merdy saw to it that I ate things in something like the right order, but she was not one to restrain a healthy appetite, which I had. However, although I ate more than anyone else, I finished first. The grown-ups would be lingering over their third or fourth cup of tea and I would be fidgeting on the mohair. At this point I was always told that I could 'get down' if I wished and go and have a sweetie.

The sweeties were kept in a decorated brown tin in the top drawer of a chest of drawers (still in my possession) in the drawing room. It was understood that, although I went in there by myself, I would have only one sweetie. Thus ended high tea. Much later, around 9.15 pm, the day would end with more tea, and tea biscuits, and I would be packed off to bed. Merdy would go to bed early too, leaving Twinko to smoke his pipe. So there are the roots of 'A Kipper with My Tea'. The kippers which Merdy bought were, or course, excellent—the fishmonger, though not a betting man, was just as good a tradesman as the butcher—but this was taken for granted, just like the excellence of the bread, the freshness of the butter and the home-laid eggs, and so on. No one went on about how the kippers had come from this or that special kipperer.

Alan Davidson
A Kipper With My Tea Macmillan (1988)

Scotch Petticoat-Tails

Mix a half-ounce (or fewer, or none) of caraway-seeds with a pound and three quarters of flour. Make a hole in the middle of the flour, and pour into it twelve ounces of butter melted in a quarter-pint of milk, and three ounces of beat sugar. Knead this, but not too much, or it will not be *short*; divide it in two, and roll it out round, rather thin. Cut out the cake by running a paste cutter round a dinner-plate, or any large round dish inverted on the paste. Cut a cake from the centre of this one with a small saucer or large tumbler. Keep this inner circle whole, and cut the outer one into eight *petticoat-tails*. Bake on paper laid on tins, serve the round cake in the middle of the plate, and the *petticoat-tails* as *radii* round it. An English traveller in Scotland, and one well acquainted with France, states in his very pleasant book that our Club have fallen into a mistake in the name of these cakes, and that *petticoat-tails* is a corruption of the French *Petites Gatelles*. It may be so: in Scottish culinary terms there are many corruptions, though we rather think the name *Petticoat-tails* has its origin in the shape of the cakes, which is exactly that of the bell-hoop petticoats of our ancient Court ladies.

Margaret Dods
The Cook and Housewife's Manual (1826)

Christian Isobel Johnstone (1781-1857) wrote *The Cook and Housewife's Manual* in 1826, using as her pseudonym Mistress Margaret (Meg) Dods, the landlady of the Cleikum Inn in Scott's novel *St Ronan's Well* (1823).

A Scotch Christmas Bun

Take four pounds of flour, keeping out a little to work it up with; make a hole in the middle of the flour, and break in sixteen ounces of butter; pour in a pint of warm water, and three gills of yeast, and work it up into a smooth dough. If it is not moist enough, put a little more warm water: then cut off one-third of the dough, and lay it aside for the cover. Take three pounds of stoned raisins, three pounds of cleaned currants, half a pound of blanched almonds cut longways; candied orange and citron peel cut, of each eight ounces; half an ounce of cloves, an ounce of cinnamon, and two ounces of ginger, all beat and sifted. Mix the spices, then spread out the dough; lay the fruit upon it; strew the spices over the fruit, and mix all together. When it is well kneaded, roll out the cover. Cover it neatly, trim it round the sides, prickle it, and bind it with paper to keep it in shape; set it in a pretty quick oven, and just before you take it out, glaze the top with a beat egg.

Margaret Dods
The Cook and Housewife's Manual (1826)

Lectio Secunda

Patriarchis, profeitis, and appostillis deir,
Confessouris, virgynis, and marteris cleir,
And all the saitt clestiall,
Devotely we upoun thame call,
That sone out of your panis fell,
Ye may in hevin heir with us dwell,
To eit swan, cran, pertrik, and plever,
And every fische that swymis in rever;
To drynk with us the new fresche wyne,
That grew upoun the rever of Ryne,
Fresche fragrant clairettis out of France,
Of Angers and of Orliance,
With mony ane cours of grit dyntie:
Say ye amen for cheritie.

William Dunbar (c.1460-1520)
The Dregy of Dunbar

William Dunbar's *Dregy* or *Dirge* extols the paradisal delights of
Edinburgh over the miseries of Stirling. As well as a song or service for
the dead, dirge also came to mean the refreshments after a funeral.

Apples

I eat an apple, skin, core, and pips,
And sleep at night the way a yokel sleeps
With thyme and borage in my palliasse,
Lavender pillows in the house of grass.

Apples of Portnauld, scarlet, round and good,
Ripened, come autumn, into savoury
Pleasures. I picked, then chewed in solitude
Behind the crumbling wall, out of the way.

I don't know why I should remember this —
Perhaps the pippin was enough to do it
With its hard flesh, delicious, bitten kiss.
I sit tonight and it is very quiet.

Douglas Dunn (b. 1942)
Northlight, Faber (1988)

Eating in Mull

The English eat very little bread; the Scots eat more: there were three different kinds used at Mr McLean's table.

The first, which may be regarded as a luxury for the country, is sea biscuit, which vessels from Glasgow sometimes leave in passing.

The second is made of oatmeal formed into unleavened dough, and then spread with a rolling pin into round cakes, about a foot in diameter and the twelfth part of an inch thick. These cakes are baked, or rather dried, on a thin plate of iron which is suspended over the fire. This is the principal bread of such as are in easy circumstances.

The third kind, which is specially appropriated to tea and breakfast, in the opulent families of the isles, consists of barley cakes, without leaven, and prepared in the same manner as the preceding, but so thin, that after spreading them over with butter, they are easily doubled into several folds; which render them very agreeable to those who are fond of this kind of dainties.

At ten in the morning, the bell announces that breakfast is on the table. All repair to the parlour, where they find a fire of peat, mixed with pit-coal, and a table elegantly served up and covered with the following articles:

Plates of smoked beef,
Cheese of the country and English cheese, in trays of mahogany,
Fresh eggs,
Salted herring,
Butter,
Milk and cream,

A sort of *bouillie*, of oatmeal and water. In eating this *bouillie*, each spoonful is plunged into a bason of cream, which is always beside it.

Milk worked up with the yolks of eggs, sugar and rum. This singular mixture is drank cold, and without being prepared by fire:

Current jelly,
Conserve of *myrtle*, a wild fruit that grows among the heath,
Tea,
Coffee,

The three sorts of bread above-mentioned;
and, Jamaica Rum.

Such is the style in which Mr McLean's breakfast table was served up every morning, while we were at his house. There was always the same abundance, with no other difference in general than in the greater or less variety of the dishes.

Dinner is put on the table at four o' clock. It consists in general of the following particulars, which I correctly noted in my journal.

1. A large dish of Scotch soup, composed of broth of beef, mutton, and sometimes fowl, mixed with a little oatmeal, onions, parsley, and a considerable quantity of pease. Instead of slices of bread small slices of mutton and the giblets of fowls are thrown into this soup.
2. Pudding of bullock's blood and barley meal, seasoned with plenty of pepper and ginger.
3. Excellent beef-steaks broiled.
4. Roasted mutton of the best quality.
5. Potatoes done in the juice of the mutton.
6. Sometimes heath-cocks, wood-cocks or water-fowl.
7. Cucumbers and ginger, pickled with vinegar.
8. Milk prepared in a variety of ways.
9. Cream and Madeira wine.
10. Pudding made of barley-meal, cream, and currants of Corinth, done up with suet.

All these various dishes appear on the table at the same time; the mistress of the house presides, and serves all round.

In a very short time the toasts commence; it is the business of the mistress to begin the ceremony. A large glass filled with port-wine is put into her hand; she drinks to the health of all the company, and passes it to one of the persons who sit next to her; and it thus proceeds from one to another round the whole table.

The side-board is furnished with three large glasses of a similar kind; of which one is appropriated to beer, another to wine, and the third to water, when it is called for in its unmixed state, which is not often. These glasses are common to all at table; they are never rinsed, but merely wiped with a fine towel after each person drinks.

The dessert, from the want of fruit, consists for the most part, only of two sorts of cheese, that of Cheshire, and what is made in the country itself.

The cloth is removed after the dessert, and the table of well polished mahogany, appears in all its lustre. It is soon covered with elegant glass decanters of English manufacture, containing port, sherry, and Madeira wines, and with capacious bowls filled with punch. Small glasses are then profusely distributed to every one.

In England, the ladies leave the table the moment the toasts begin. The custom is not precisely the same here; they remain at least half an hour after, and justly partake in the festivity of a scene, in which formality being laid aside, Scottish frankness and kindness have full room to display themselves. It is certain that the men are benefited by this intercourse, and the ladies are nothing the losers by it.

At Mr McLean's we drank in particular to each of the ladies present.

To the rest of the guests, mentioning their names one by one.

To the country.

To liberty.

To the happiness of mankind in general.

To friendship.

We, foreigners, drank more than once to our good friends the Highlanders; and the company answered in full chorus with drinking to our friends in France, and in a lower tone, with a glass of mild Madeira, to our mistresses.

The ladies then left us for a little to prepare the tea. They returned in about half an hour after; and the servants followed them with coffee, small tarts, butter, milk, and tea. Music, conversation, reading the news, though a little old by the time they reach this, and walking, when the weather permits, fill up the remainder of the evening; and thus the time passes quickly away. But it is somewhat unpleasant to be obligated to take one's seat at the table again about ten o' clock, and remain until mid-night over supper nearly of the same fare as the dinner, and in no less abundance.

Such is the life which the richer classes lead in a country, where there is not even a road, where not a tree is to be seen, the mountains being covered only with heath, where it rains for eight months of the year, and where the sea is in a state of perpetual convulsion.

B. Faujas Saint-Fond (1741-1819)
Travels in England, Scotland and the Hebrides, London (1799)

To The Principal and Professors
of the University of St Andrews
on their Superb Treat to Dr Samuel Johnson

St Andrews town may look right gawsy,
Nae grass will grow upon her cawsey,
Nor wa'-flowers of a yellow dye,
Glour dowy o'er her ruins high,
Sin Samy's head weel pang'd wi' lear,
Has seen the *Alma Mater* there:
Regents, my winsome billy boys!
'Bout him you've made an unco noise;
Nae doubt for him your bells wad clink
To find him upon Eden's brink,
An' a' things nicely set in order,
Wad kep him on the Fifan border:
I'se warrant now frae France an' Spain,
Baith cooks and scullions mony ane
Wad gar the pats an' kettles tingle
Around the college kitchen ingle,
To fleg frae a' your craigs the roup,
Wi' reeking het and crieshy soup;
And snails and puddocks mony hunder
Wad beeking lie the hearth-stane under,
Wi' roast and boild, an' a' kin kind,
To heat the body, cool the mind.

But hear me lads! gin I'd been there,
How I wad trimm'd the bill o' fare!
For ne'er sic surly wight as he
Had met wi' sic respect frae me.
Mind ye what Sam, the lying loun!
Has in his Dictionar laid down?
That aits in England are a feast
To cow an' horse, an' sican beast,
While in Scots ground this growth was common
To gust the gab o' man and woman.
Tak tent, ye Regents! then, an' hear

My list o' gudely hamel gear,
Sic as ha'e often rax'd the wyme
O' blyther fallows mony time;
Mair hardy, souple, steive an' swank,
Than ever stood on Samy's shank.

Imprimis, then, a haggis fat,
Weel tottled in a seything pat,
Wi' spice and ingans weel ca'd thro',
Had help'd to gust the stirrah's mow,
And plac'd itsel in truncher clean
Before the gilpy's glowrin een.

Secundo, then a gude sheep's head
Whase hide was singit, never flead,
And four black trotters cled wi' girsle,
Bedown his throat had learn'd to hirsle.

What think ye neist, o' gude fat brose
To clag his ribs? a dainty dose!
And white and bloody puddins routh,
To gar the Doctor skirl, O Drouth!
Whan he cou'd never houp to merit
A cordial o' reaming claret,
But thraw his nose, and brize and pegh
O'er the contents o' sma' ale quegh:
Then let his wisdom girn and snarl
O'er a weel-tostit girdle farl,
An' learn, that maugre o' his wame,
Ill bairns are ay best heard at hame.

Drummond, lang syne, o' Hawthornden,
The wyliest an' best o' men,
Has gi'en you dishes ane or mae,
That wad ha' gard his grinders play,
Not to *roast beef*, old England's life,
But to the auld *east nook of Fife*,
Whare Creilian crafts cou'd weel ha'e gi'en

Scate-rumples to ha'e clear'd his een;
Than neist whan Samy's heart was faintin,
He'd lang'd for scate to mak him wanton.

Ah! willawins, for Scotland now,
Whan she maun stap ilk birky's mow
Wi' eistacks, grown as 'tware in pet
In foreign land, or green-house het,
When cog o' brose an' cutty spoon
Is a' our cottar childer's boon,
Wha thro' the week, till Sunday's speal,
Toil for pease-clods an' gude lang kail.
Devall then, Sirs, and never send
For daintiths to regale a friend,
Or, like a torch at baith ends burning,
Your house'll soon grow mirk and mourning.

What's this I hear some cynic say?
Robin, ye loun! its nae fair play;
Is there nae ither subject rife
To clap your thumb upon but Fife?
Gi'e o'er, young man, you'll meet your corning,
Than caption war, or charge o' horning;
Some canker'd surly sour-mow'd carline
Bred near the abbey o' Dumfarline,
Your shoulders yet may gi'e a lounder,
An' be of verse the mal-confounder.

Come on, ye blades! but 'ere ye tulzie,
Or hack our flesh wi' sword or gulzie,
Ne'er shaw your teeth, nor look like stink,
Nor o'er an empty bicker blink:
What weets the wizen an' the wyme,
Will mend your prose and heal my rhyme.

Robert Fergusson (1750-74)
in *Poems by Allan Ramsay and Robert Fergusson,*
Scottish Academic Press and ASLS (1985)

from 'Caller Oysters'

Whan big as burns the butters rin,
Gin ye hae catcht a droukit skin,
To *Luckie Middlemist's* loup in,
    And sit fu snug
Oe'r oysters and a dram o' gin,
    Or haddock lug.

While glakit fools, o'er rife o' cash,
Pamper their weyms wi' fousom trash,
I think a chiel may gayly pass;
    He's no ill boden
That gusts his gabb wi' oyster sauce,
    And *hen* weel soden.

Robert Fergusson
'Caller Oysters', *Weekly Magazine* 27 Aug 1772

A genuine oyster-eater rejects all additions—wine, eschalott,
lemon, etc., are alike obnoxious to his taste for the native juice.

Margaret Dods
The Cook and Housewife's Manual (1826)

Ian Hamilton Finlay

A Peach/An Apple

a peach
   an apple
      a table
 an eatable
  peach
   an apple
     an eatable
      table
     apple
   an apple
    a peach

Ian Hamilton Finlay (b. 1925)
Poems to Hear and See, Macmillan (1971)

Clapshot

In those bygone days, especially in harvest, potatoes were served for breakfast, dinner and supper, as there was often very little meal until the crop was cut. For breakfast the potatoes were boiled with the skins on. When cooked, they were "sied" (strained), peeled and put back in the pot hanging over the fire. After the peeling was completed, a little oatmeal and salt were sprinkled over them, and they were mashed and supped out of the pot, either sweet-milk or kirnmilk being served with them. For dinner the potatoes were boiled with their jackets on, and when cooked, they were poured in a large basin—usually the "baking plate"—or "cooped" (emptied) in the middle of the table. A bowl containing "dippings" (melted fat or butter) was placed in the centre of the heap. The family gathered round, each one peeled for himself and dipped in the fat, neither spoon nor fork being used. When possible to obtain dog-fish from Orphir or Birsay, it was dried, and, either boiled or roasted on the girdle, it formed a tasty accompaniment to the potatoes. Instead of a second course, or as a pudding, thick kirnmilk and meal was served, or as a special treat, "louts" (that is sour clotted sweet-milk) and "burstin". For supper, kail or turnips boiled with pared potatoes were mashed together, and, well savoured with salt and pepper, eaten with bere bannocks. This vegetarian dish bore the curious name of "clapshot."

John Firth
Reminiscences of An Orkney Parish,
Orkney Natural History Society (1974)

Graham Fulton

Pandora's Box of Maltesers

Outside
the ALL-NIGHT Cinema
with stuffing sweating from razored seats
people are driving home to their beds.

Inside
the ALL-NIGHT Cinema
full of dark and finger-fucking and farts
we settle down to watch PLAGUE OF THE ZOMBIES.

The horror around us breathes in.
We open a box of Maltesers.
The tear-your-ticket-in-half girl
yawns,
shines
a light into
our eyes,
wanders back up
the carpet aisle.

Dream-sequence zombies stumble about
with egg white eyes and dressed in sacks.
The cold sucks in our toes,
pastes itself
onto
our
skin
(but we'll be home in an hour
or six.)

Inside
the ALL-NIGHT Cinema
fat with whispered threats and cider shouts
the homeless children curl up for the night
inside their jumpers
and shirts.

Glasgow around us breathes out.
We settle down to watch LUST FOR A VAMPIRE,
open
a box of
Smarties.

Graham Fulton (b. 1959)
Scream if you want to go faster, ASLS (1991)

Besides such homely sweets as gundy, glessie, cheugh jeans and
black man, there were bottles of 'boilings' (Scotch Mixtures) that
glittered like rubies, emeralds, topazes and all the jewels of the
Orient, and tasted of all of the fruits of the orchard and spices of
the Indies.

F. Marian McNeill
The Scots Kitchen, Blackie (1929)

Picnic

Solid enough to resist the wear and tear of time,
the Castle is built on solid quartz slate, its steep
face reflected in the Maine. The Chapel was
transformed into a military and civil prison which
once housed 200 English sailors. In 1815 it was
occupied by Prussians then used as a munitions
store in WW2, evacuated by the Germans just
before the first Allied bombardment. Even so, the
roofs and a vault in the chapel were subjected to
direct hits and destroyed; the restoration work you
see today was carried out after the liberation. The
unobtrusive modern Gallery housing the
remarkable Tapestry of the Apocalypse was
opened in July 1954: the garden in the French style
in 1948.

The garden was too hot as well. Of course it was. Rona had chosen a
specially hot bit. Even the bench: slats cooking the arse as you sat. Cassie
rummaged in her bag. The suncream tube was flaccid, unhealthily warm.
Even through the layers of the canvas bag. Cassie placed the nozzle on
her upper arm, squeezing. A fat white worm oozed out, viscous solids
separating from a surround of clear stuff. Like creamed suet. Cassie didn't
care. She rubbed it over the too-warm skin surface, trying not to hear it
crackle.

Phlox. Phlox paniculata.

Cassie turned round and back again not looking. Her fingers were
sticky.

You didn't see it, Rona said. Look. The stuff I've got out the back door
near the whirly. The pink flowers.

I can't look. I need a tissue Rona. Tissues.

Rona patted one shorts' pocket then the other. A flattened scroll
emerged from the second. Here, she said. Here.

Three rolled together. Cassie used them one at a time, rubbing
between her fingers. Rona sighed and looked back at the plants.

There. They've got it three colours. I could get some for that window-box you've got. Put something in it that isn't dead. What do you think?

I'm starving. Can we eat yet?

Cassie crushed the tissues into a ball inside one palm, holding it there. No pockets. Rona sighed, took the tissue debris and put it back into the shorts' pocket.

Like talking to a filing cabinet. You couldn't care less, could you?

She hauled two bags out from under the seat. Rona handed over the brown one.

Here. Make yourself useful.

Half a white cob loaf, a brown poke mushy in one corner, two separate bits of cheese wrapped in paper, two tubs of mango yoghurt and an empty tube of paper off an absent bar of chocolate. Cassie put them in a neat line. Rona hauled a flask out and set it upright near the bread. The hellish blue flask with the spare cup. Rona anchored a polythene poke under one of the bits of cheese and said For rubbish, darkly. Cassie said nothing. A cherry fell out of the mush-cornered poke, bleeding. One of the cheese wrappings had uncurled, showing a pale yellow wedge weeping under a greyish crust. Rona looked as well. She looked for a full minute, raking for something then emptied out the rest of the bag. A rainmate, three prunes, four pens with THIS BELONGS TO RONA stickers, specs, stamps, travellers' cheques, nail clippers, indigestion tablets, receipts, used paper hankies and a saved-up Dutch biscuit she'd been given free with a cup of coffee in Byres Road. The other bag offered three sets of keys, a penknife, two passports, empty film drums, another pair of specs, the Chartres guidebook, two plastic knives, postcards, map, saved-up sugar sachets, Oxfam recycling labels, a rubber shaped like a rabbit, more receipts, an address book, a wool band and lots of blue fluff. She looked and sighed.

Never mind. We can drink it.

She meant the yoghurt.

Cassie made token gestures though she knew she didn't have a spoon either. Novel. Lip salve and the suncream, two pens and spare film. A comb and a tin of sweeties they'd bought by accident on the ferry. The tin had pine trees on the lid. Cassie had seen them and thought they meant pine as in fresh as in mint. They didn't. They meant pine as in toilet cleaner. Dettol-flavoured, shaped like Yeti's feet. Rona had said not to throw them away in case. Cassie put the tin back into the bag with the rest of her things. The novel was no temptation in this heat. Rona repacked her stuff except for the guide. She pulled a piece of brie off the end of the wedge and sucked it, angling for the light on her face.

MIght as well work on a tan.

The guide to the wrong place lay at her elbow, CHARTRES glaring up in white.

Cassie tore a piece off the loaf. People went past the end of the garden pointing at grass and birds. Cassie watched, chewing. No-one else was eating bread. No-one else had carrier-bags or rows of food melting in the sun. A hot rubber smell suddenly filled out under Cassie's nose. Rona holding up the flask. Cassie could see an old couple advancing behind Rona's back, a child between, holding their hands. Rona held up the thermos. Chipped Tippex that had once read RONA'S still clung grimy white on the neck. Rona raised the thing like a wine bottle, looked quizzical. A stain on her T-shirt. Again.

Cassie and Rona

Rona and Cassie

have eaten sandwiches in Amsterdam and Gouda, Copenhagen, York, Warsaw, Munich and Lerwick, under trees, in fields, off the side of main roads on steps to bowling alleys and cinemas and in the shadow of the reat oran of Haarlem. It's what we always do. We get no richer, no more sophisticated, no more included. We know our place: that proper holidays are for proper people with proper money and that real travellers, in denim bermudas of uneven leg length, travel to real faraway places in search of real poor people enduring real life in the raw. We are neither real nor proper: just fraudulent moochers in other people's territory, getting by on the cheap.

Cassie watched a small pebble, rubbed smooth like beach glass, near her foot on the path. Individual strands of grass rimming the path border. The shadows of the old couple's shoes drew level, walked past. A moment later, the child's, little bites of breath on each downtread, running. Out of eyeshot, someone laughed. Trying to stifle the sound but laughing anyway. It was quite clear. Cassie tilted her head sideways. Rona was pouring another half cup from the flask, sipped, sniffed, wiped her nose with the back of her hand then turned to look out, her forehead smooth, into a place higher than Cassie allowed herself to see.

That's nice as well. That buddleia. I'm definitely getting a buddleia when we get back.

She waved one sandal-free foot in the air, smiling at nothing at all. Rona, inside the jewel case of roughly beautiful walls and towers with an unobtrusive modern gallery housing the remarkable Tapestry of the Apocalypse. The Imperturbable, Queen of All She Surveyed.

Janice Galloway (b. 1956)
Foreign Parts, Cape (1994)

We lay upon the bare top of a rock like scones upon a girdle.

Robert Louis Stevenson
Kidnapped (1886)

Scottish Fare

Miss Girzy laughed as she retired to execute the order, while her mother continued, as she had done from the first introduction, to inspect Claud from head to foot, with a curious and something of a suspicious eye; there was even an occasional flush that gleamed through the habitual paleness of her thoughtful countenance, redder and warmer than the hectic glow of mere corporeal indisposition. Her attention, however, was soon drawn to the spacious round table in the middle of the room, by one of the maids entering with a large pewter tureen, John Drappie, the man-servant, having been that morning sent on some caption and horning business of the laird's to Gabriel Beagle, the Kilmarnock lawyer. But, as the critics hold it indelicate to describe the details of any refectionary supply, however elegant, we must not presume to enumerate the series and succession of Scottish fare which soon crowned the board, all served on pewter as bright as plate. Our readers must endeavour, by the aid of their own fancies, to form some idea of the various forms in which the head and harigals of the sheep that had been put to death for the occasion were served up, not forgetting the sonsy, savoury, sappy haggis, together with the gude fat hen, the float whey, which, in a large china punchbowl, graced the centre of the table, and supplied the place of jellies, tarts, tartlets, and puddings.

John Galt (1779-1839)
The Entail (1822)

Invite

University of Edinburgh
School of Scottish Studies
17 January 1972

Dear Sir, or Madam, as the case may be,
We request the pleisure of yir companee
At the

21ST BIRTHDAY PARTY

of the Schule of Scottish Studies

DRESS INFORMAL i.e. the usual orra duddies,

ON THE 29TH JANUAR AT 7 P. M.

Sae ye can easy get there efter the gemm.
We'd better tell ye, no to be mair circumstantial,
That ye'll maist likely get something gey substantial,
For beit said, the Schule of Scottish Studies
Kens mair about cookery than jist hou to byle tatties
                              and haddies,
There's to be Haggis and Clapshot, Stapag, and
                              parritch caad Brochan,
That thick, ye'll maybe can tak some o't hame in yir
                              spleughan,
Atholl Brose, very nice, to mak yir thochts mair
                              effervescent,
Frae a genuine Atholl recipe—we mean the Forest,
                              no the Crescent.

R. S. V. P. BY THURSDAY, 27TH JAN.

Robert Garioch (1909-81)
A Scottish Postbag edited by George Bruce and Paul H. Scott,
Edinburgh (1986)

Scotch Broth

'Intae this,' commanded the receipt, 'fling a sma' haunfie o' coorse saut. Whan it biles pit in yer beef, a guid, fat, twa-pun piece. Then hauf-a-pun o' weel-washed baurley and twa pun o' well-soakit peas.' About ten-thirty Andra added 'wan guid swede turmut, fower carrots, eicht guid leeks and a wee tait o' sugar.' Before departing for his 'bit dram' he added 'twa guid haunfies o' choppit greens and eicht tautties'; and on his return—exuding the rich and heady perfume of the Special, he stirred in another 'haunfie'—this time of parsley which, with canny fore-thought—he had chopped before setting forth.

Madeline Gibb
Scotland's Magazine (December 1960)

Lucky Laing . . . contrived to make her shop in the gloomy old Tolbooth a cosy little place, half tavern, half kitchen, whence issued pretty frequently the pleasant sounds of broiling beef-steaks, and the drawing of corks from bottles of ale and porter.

Marie W. Stuart
Old Edinburgh Taverns (1952)

Chris's Wedding

So down she went, folk had trooped back in the parlour by then and were sitting them round the tables, the minister at the head of one, Long Rob at the head of another, in the centre one the wedding cake stood tall on its stand with the Highland dirk beside it that Ewan had gotten from McIvor to do the cutting. The wind had risen storming without as Chris stood to cut, there in her blue frock with the long, loose sleeves, there came a great whoom in the chimney and some looked out at the window and said that the drifts would be fell feet deep by the morn.

The minister had thawed away by then, he was laughing real friendly-like in his bull-like boom of a voice, telling of other weddings he'd made in his time, they'd all been gey funny and queer-like weddings, things that you laughed at, not fine like this. And Chris listened and glowed with pride that everything at hers was just and right; and then again as so often that qualm of doubt came down on her, separating her away from these kindly folk of the farms—kind, and aye ready to believe the worst of others they heard, unbelieving that others could think the same of themselves. So maybe the minister no more than buttered her, she looked at him with the dark, cool doubt in her face, next instant forgot him in glow of remembrance that blinded all else: she was married to Ewan.

Beside her: he whispered *Oh, eat something, Chris, you'll fair go famished*, and she tried some ham and a bit of the dumpling, sugared and fine, that Mistress Melon had made. And everybody praised it, as well they might, and cried for more helpings, and more cups of tea, and there were scones and pancakes and soda-cakes and cakes made with honey that everybody ate; and little Wat Strachan stopped eating of a sudden and cried *Mother, I'm not right in the belly!* everybody laughed at that but Kirsty, she jumped to her feet and hurried him out, and came back with him with his face real frightened. But faith! It didn't put a stop to the bairn, he started in again as hungry as ever, and Chae cried out *Well, well, let him be, maybe it tasted as fine coming up as it did going down!*

Lewis Grassic Gibbon (1901-35)
Sunset Song, Jarrolds (1932)

Lewis Grassic Gibbon

An Aberdeen High Tea

High tea in Aberdeen is like no other meal on earth. It is the meal of the day, the meal par excellence, and the tired come home to it ravenous, driven by the granite streets, hounded in for energy to stoke against that menace. Tea is drunk with the meal, and the order of it is this: First, one eats a plateful of sausages and eggs and mashed potatoes; then a second plateful to keep down the first. Eating, one assists the second plateful to its final home by mouthfuls of oatcake spread with butter. Then you eat oatcakes with cheese. Then there are scones. Then cookies. Then it is really time to begin on tea—tea and bread and butter and crumpets and toasted rolls and cakes. Then some Dundee cake. Then—about half-past seven—someone shakes you out of the coma into which you have fallen and asks you persuasively if you wouldn't like another cup of tea and just *one* more egg and sausage. . . .

And all night long, on top of this supper and one of those immense Aberdonian beds which appear to be made of knotted ship's cable, the investigator, through and transcending the howl of the November sleet-wind, will hear the lorries and drays, in platoons, clattering up and down Market Street. They do it for no reason or purpose, except to keep you awake. And in the morning when you descend with a grey face and an aching head, they provide you with an immense Aberdeen breakfast; and if you halt and gasp somewhere through the third course they send for the manager who comes and questions you gravely as to why you don't like the food?—should he send for a doctor?

Lewis Grassic Gibbon
Scottish Scene, Jarrolds (1934)

Innocence

In the days afore the war
The teas were the thing
At oor hoose.
Kitchened mince collops
Wi doughbaas, and breid
Soakit and sappy
In wattery gravy. Or black puddins
Horse-shoe anes tied wi a string
And made as anerlie MacDonal*
Kent hoo. Or the treat
O fried tatties kept frae
Dinner.
—And me but a gutsy loon.

In the days atween the wars
The teas were the thing
At oor hoose.
Thin sheaves o fried breid
Brouned and crisp on
Baith sides
Or jeelie-pieces; thick
Door-step anes wi the jam
Rinnin aff the marg.
And scones: tattie scones;
Soda scones; or treacle
Scones.
—And faither oot o a job.

* Ramsay MacDonald & Co.

In the days afore the war
The teas were the thing
At oor hoose.
Pancakes richt frae the girdle
And gane afore the butter
Richt haurdened.
And ginger breid: "Best withoot
Butter or cream". And aye
A great joog o soor-dook
To gae wi it aa, frae the cairt
Comin special at fower
O'clock.
—Wi mither in the queue.

In the days afore the war
The teas were the thing
At oor hoose.
Cream cookies; braw sugar-tapped
Anes wi the cream oozed oot
For lickin.
And biscuits to finish:
Perkins, bannocks mebbe,
And e'en the haurd Empire
Biscuits wi reid toories on
The icin.
—And me but a growein loon.

Duncan Glen (b. 1933)
Selected Poems 1965-1990,
Akros Publications (1991)

The River Bank

The Mole waggled his toes from sheer happiness, spread his chest with a sigh of full contentment, and leaned back blissfully into the soft cushions. "*What* a day I'm having!" he said. "Let us start at once!"

"Hold hard a minute, then!" said the Rat. He looped the painter through a ring in his landing-stage, climbed up into his hole above, and after a short interval reappeared staggering under a fat, wicker luncheon-basket.

"Shove that under your feet," he observed to the Mole, as he passed it down into the boat. Then he untied the painter and took the sculls again.

"What's inside it?" asked the Mole, wriggling with curiosity.

"There's cold chicken inside it," replied the Rat briefly; "coldtongue-coldhamcoldbeefpickledgherkinssaladfrenchrollscresssandwidges-pottedmeatgingerbeerlemonadesodawater—"

"O stop, stop," cried the Mole in ecstasies: "This is too much!"

"Do you really think so?" inquired the Rat seriously. "It's only what I always take on these little excursions; and the other animals are always telling me that I'm a mean beast and cut it *very* fine!"

Kenneth Grahame (1859-1932)
The Wind in the Willows, Methuen (1908)

I want a plain ham-and-egg tea . . . and some cookies and cakes.

R. M. Williamson, *Scotland*, *Readings etc.*
edited T. W. Paterson (1929)

Elizabeth Grant

Bainne Briste

The Captain and Mrs Grant lived in the low parlour to the left of the entrance, within which was a light closet in which they slept; the hall was flagged, but a strip of home-made carpet covered the centre, of the same pattern as that in the parlour, a check of black and green. The parlour curtain was home-made too of linsey-woolsey, red and yellow. A good peat fire burned on the hearth; a rug knit by Mrs Grant kept the fire-place tidy. A round mahogany table was placed against the wall, with a large japanned tray standing up on end on it; several hair-bottomed chairs were ranged all round. A japanned corner-cupboard fixed on a bracket at some height from the floor very much ornamented the room, as it was filled with the best tall glasses on their spiral stalks, and some china too fine for use; a number of silver-edged punch-ladles, and two silver edged and silver-lined drinking-horns were presented to full view on the lowest shelf, and outside upon the very top was a large china punchbowl. But the cupboard we preferred was in the wall next the fire. It was quite a pantry; oatcakes, barley scones, flour scones, butter, honey, sweetmeats, cheese, and wine, and spiced whisky, all came out of the deep shelves of this agreeable recess, as did the great key of the dairy; this was often given to one of us to carry to old Mary the cook, with leave to see her skim and whip the fine rich cream, which Mrs Grant would afterwards pour on a whole pot of jam and give us for luncheon. This dish, under the name of 'bainne briste,' or broken milk, is a great favourite wherever it has been introduced.

Elizabeth Grant of Rothiemurchus (1797-1885)
Memoirs of a Highland Lady (1899)

Shepherd's Pie

Someone told Mrs Thaw that the former tenants of her flat had killed themselves by putting their head in the oven and turning the gas on. She wrote at once to the corporation asking that her gas cooker be changed for an electric one, but as Mr Thaw would still need food when he returned from work she baked him a shepherd's pie, but with her lips more tightly pursed than usual.

Her son always refused shepherd's pie or any other food whose appearance disgusted him: spongy white tripe, soft penis-like sausages, stuffed sheep's hearts with their valves and little arteries. When one of these came before him he poked it uncertainly with his fork and said, "I don't want it."

"Why not?"

"It looks queer."

"But you havnae tasted it! Taste just a week bit. For my sake."

"No."

"Children in China are starving for food like that."

"Send it to them."

After more discussion his mother would say in a high-pitched voice, "You'll sit at this table till you eat every bit" or "Just you wait till I tell your father about this, my dear." Then he would put a piece of food in his mouth, gulp without tasting it and vomit it back onto the plate. After that he would be shut in the back bedroom. Sometimes his mother came to the door and said, "Will you not eat just a wee bit of it? For my sake?" then Thaw, feeling cruel, shouted "No" and went to the window and looked down into the back green. He would see friends playing there, or the midden-rakers, or neighbours hanging out washing, and feel so lonely and magnificent that he considered opening the window and jumping out. It was a bitter glee to imagine his corpse thudding to the ground among them. At last, with terror, he would hear his father coming *clomp-clomp* upstairs, carrying his bicycle. Usually Thaw ran to meet him. Now he heard his mother open the door, the mutter of voices in conspiracy, then footsteps coming to the bedroom and his mother whispering, "Don't hurt him too much."

Mr Thaw would enter with a grim look and say, "Duncan! You've behaved badly to your mother again. She goes to the bother and expense of making a good dinner and ye won't eat it. Aren't ye ashamed of yourself?."

Thaw would hang his head.

"I want you to apologize to her."

"Don't know what 'polgize means."

"Tell her you're sorry and you'll eat what you are given."

Then Thaw would snarl "No, I won't!" and be thrashed.

During the thrashing he screamed a lot and afterward stamped, yelled, tore his hair and banged his head against the wall until his parents grew frightened and Mr Thaw shouted, "Stop that or I'll draw my hand off yer jaw!"

Then Thaw beat his own face with his fist, screaming, "Like this like this like *this*?"

It was hard to silence him without undoing the justice of the punishment. On the advice of a neighbour they one day undressed the furiously kicking boy, filled a bath with cold water and plunged him in. The sudden chilling scald destroyed all his protest and this treatment was used on later occasions with equal success. Shivering slightly he would be dried with soft towels before the living-room fire, then put to bed with his doll. Before sleep came he lay stunned and emotionless while his mother tucked him in. Sometimes he considered withholding the goodnight kiss but could never quite manage it.

When he had been punished for not eating a particular food he was not given that food again but a boiled egg instead. Yet after hearing how the former tenants had misused their oven he looked very thoughtfully at the shepherd's pie when it was brought to table that evening. At length he pointed and said, "Can I have some?"

Mrs Thaw looked at her husband and took her spoon and plonked a dollop onto Thaw's plate. He stared at the mushy potato with particles of carrot, cabbage and mince in it and wondered if brains really looked like that. Fearfully he put some in his mouth and churned it with his tongue. It tasted good so he ate what was on the plate and asked for more. When the meal was over his mother said, "There. You like it. Aren't you ashamed of kicking up all that din about nothing?"

Alasdair Gray (b. 1934)
Lanark, Canongate (1981)

Puffins

He now drew himself up on his breast until he faced the burrow. Swathing his right hand in his bonnet, he thrust it tentatively into the shallow burrow. Out came a parrot beak. Down came Finn's left, swift as a beast's paw, and caught the head. A twist and a pull, and the bird was dead. In went his right hand, and the fingers touched, closed gently upon, and drew forth an egg, whitish in colour, with vague ashen spots. He gazed upon its miracle of beauty. It was warm. He shook it by its ear. It was firm. He picked up a sharp pebble from the mouth of the burrow and cracked a hole in each end of the egg. He sniffed, introduced the pointed end to his mouth, and sucked. Slimy, soft as velvet, came the white; a pause, and the yolk broke along his palate in a wave, a choking fullness, a rich gluttony; more wet velvet, and his breath whistled inward through the vacant holes. He regarded the empty shell with a slow smile and tossed it over the edge to play with the wind. His eyes turned, searching for burrows. Most of them were arm-deep, and when a bird shoved out its egg to meet his hand, swathed in his bonnet, he could not help laughing.

In a little while, he was walking towards the boat, with bottles of water, three dead puffins, and twelve eggs in his round bonnet. As he hove in sight, it was almost ludicrous to see how the four faces were gazing up.

Roddie held to his course.

Soon the flat land of Lewis was clear stretching far to the north, but not until they could see the waters white against the great headlands did Roddie bear away. "I think, boys," he said, "we'll try for the Butt."

The wind was now almost dead astern and the going easier. It was well to be done with this ocean! The wind, too, was taking off. Within an hour, Roddie had the reefs out, driving the *Seafoam* all he could. Finn saw the stem lifting and racing, eager now to realize its own wooden dream. If Roddie took a risk he would be ready with a counter. And that stem would help him!

"What about your eggs now, Finn?" asked Callum.

Finn took the four eggs and offered the first one to Roddie.

"There's not one for us all," said Roddie reasonably.

"I wish you would take it," said Finn, his expression darkening.

"Thanks," said Roddie. "Will you break two holes in the end for me?"

This Finn did, and then he handed an egg to each of the others.

"What about yourself?" asked Callum.

"The thought of it still makes me want to spew," said Finn, smiling. "I had four. This is only your third."

"Good health !" said Rob.

"Your very good health!" said Callum.

Henry raised his egg. Roddie nodded and glanced back over his shoulder. Finn felt embarrassed and very happy.

In the late evening they rounded the Butt, but well to seaward to avoid the broken tumult, and as they came into the quiet waters of the Minch they looked about them with marvelling humoured eyes.

Roddie steered into a little creek and ran her foot upon the sand in a slow hiss.

When Callum landed he staggered and fell. They all staggered, for they were weak and light-headed. A trickle of water came down into the creek, forming little pools higher up. "Don't drink too much," said Roddie.

Finn and Henry went up over the rise, and in less than an hour returned bearing an iron pot between them and a tin pail in Finn's left hand. On the tongue of sward by the strand the others watched and waited.

"It's hot porridge," said Henry.

"And a small drop of milk," said Finn.

"Take off your bonnets, boys," said Callum. "Roddie, say the grace."

Simply and sincerely Roddie said the "Grace before Meat". Their hearts were filled; and their stomachs were softly and divinely poulticed.

Neil Gunn (1891-1973)
The Silver Darlings,
Faber and Faber (1941)

Stealing Totties

Desperado though I was, my morals were offended by the sight of two boys pelting past McBride and Black's the grocer's shop and scooping up potatoes as they ran, from a basket of spuds displayed outside the shop to lure the customers. I ran into the shop like a true Wesleyan Hall boy and told the man, but he refused to give chase. "We'll no' miss a tottie or two," he said callously. When I went back out, aggrieved, I found the thieves had dislodged several other potatoes, so I picked one up and trailed after them. What kind of thing to steal was a potato? What could you do with it? It wasn't the tottie-gun season and you can't chew a murphy raw.

They were mending a road in Cubie Street, and the robbers were crouched beside the tar-boiler. Underneath it, the road was sprinkled with ashes and hot embers raked out from the boiler fire, and among the embers were the stolen potatoes, and here was I with a potato of my own. I threw it under beside theirs and gave up my principles. The only thing that went wrong with that escapade was that my potato roasted better than theirs did, and one of them claimed it as his own in exchange for a very inferior piece of cuisine he had already started eating. But there's something about a tottie roasted under a tar-boiler; something no home-cooked potato can compete with. Some day I'll get enough money to buy an old tar-boiler of my own and hire somebody to steal me a few potatoes from McBride and Black's. I still feel cheated of that potato.

Cliff Hanley (b. 1928)
Dancing in the Streets,
Hutchinson (1958)

The Menu

I live to eat—and creatively eat to live.

For me, food can never just be fodder to fill the gaping hole or a comfort crunch or, simply and essentially, fuel. How boring.

How insulting to the Pantry of Life.

My first thoughts on waking are not "Today I *will* get to the desk *immediately* on rising. . . ." or "Today I *will* write my Will. . . . " or "Today I *must* clean the loo/the flue/the henhouse. . . . " etc.

No, I deliciously muse on what I will have for supper that night before my head even leaves the pillow. The success of the day's activities is inexorably wound up and around this focus. Breakfast and lunch are but light hitching posts en route, prettily served.

Whether alone, sometimes especially then, or with family and friends at home, visiting or travelling, the evening ritual of gourmandising sets the ultimate seal of approval on life's purpose.

I once lived in a campervan for six months, continuously travelling through the islands of the Hebrides, sketching, writing, absorbing all I saw and heard. And eating . . . naturally. Each waking thought no different from the norm but with the added bonus of victualling the ritual from the land, wildly. Village stores, local produce and inter-island mainland supermarkets providing the basics—and wine.

Culinary preparation, hunched à la Notre Dame until I got the knack of elevating the campervan roof, were no less elaborate than at home.

In fact is that not the foreplay to the feast?

Whilst on Harris the first of the equinoctial gales grounded the van for several days in the Northton dunes. Salt spray from the churning Sound of Harris seeped into the engine. It was impossible to lift the bonnet and administer the elixir of WD40 until the Force 9 backed and died.

The incessant roar of wind and sea, the violent rocking of the van and the never ending blackness of the nights were evil and scary.

Come the calm after the storm I moved the van to a more sheltered hollow facing northwards to the calmer stretches of Luskentyre sands. I hadn't had a cooked meal for days, too terrified to light the little gas stove in case the van should coup. That night I dined in style, celebrating my survival.

The Menu

Lightly poached Raasay Chanterelles
in Orange Sauce on Toast

Olive oil sautéed Aubergine, slow stewed in red wine,
with Waternish mint and Glendale potatoes

Waternish Hydroponic Cherry Tomatoes
Northton Cos Lettuce

Colonsay Honey Dip

The guests in elegant Scarista House Hotel, just opposite over the bay,
could not have dined better though they had more elbow room.

Mairi Hedderwick (b. 1939)
An Eye on the Hebrides; an Illustrated Journey, Canongate (1989)

. . . bannock and a shave of cheese
Will make a breakfast that a laird might please.

Allan Ramsay (1682-1758)

Sausages

Beside Jake, on the draining board, there were some uncooked sausages lying on the grill pan. Mat looked at them and felt the saliva trickle in his mouth but he drew at the cigarette to alleviate the hunger pangs.

"Oot the road," he said to Jake. "If you let me in to the sink, I'll fill the kettle for a cuppa."

After Mat had filled the kettle and lit the gas under it he squeezed past the table and sat down on the divan which was against the wall opposite the fireplace. It was only when he sat down that he realised how tired he was from walking about. He also felt a bit light headed and dizzy from hunger. Helen got up and put the sausages on the grill. All this time Jetta had hardly acknowledged his entry but went on talking to Helen.

"You'll not be havin' to strain things for the wee fella any more."

"No. I've stopped that for a while now. He's old enough now."

They went on talking about baby-feeding. Jake moved away from the draining board to flick the long column of ash from his cigatette into the fireplace then he came over and sat on the far edge of the divan from Mat.

"Aye," he said. "Things are quite busy. Doin' well. Some of the blokes are asking after you—why don't you come in and see us oftener?"

During the last few weeks when Mat had been particularly worried or hungry he had had vivid images of himself back working in the slaughter-house, with his kit on, early in the mornings, drinking cups of scalding tea from a can and eating rolls and eggs, or skinning down a head, or slitting a tripe, or smoking cigarettes on a full stomach.

"Ah, well. Been busy."

"Aye." Jake paused for a moment and Mat could see that he was embarrassed. "How's it comin' on, I mean your—writing?"

It was as if, Mat thought, he was asking after some embarrassing seceret. It was the first time that Jake had ever asked him this question. Yet Mat shared his embarrassment, and he simply turned his head away and shrugged. "All right."

When Helen got up again and went over to the grill she spoke to Jetta saying, "I think we'll have some supper." Mat felt a moment of wild panic for he knew that their whole economy was so finely balanced that this would either wreck the whole thing or that there would be nothing in the cupboard to offer them. He got up and squeezed past the table and opened the cupboard himself. The first thing he saw was the fat packet of sugar, then the block of butter, the mince lying in a bowl, the streaky bacon gleaming through the grease-proof paper. Mat turned and looked at Helen then he went back and sat down on the couch. As soon as he had seen the packed cupboard he knew it was Jake and his mother who had brought the things and that it would have been Jake who would have paid for them. With the amount of fasting Mat had done recently his senses had sharpened. He had smelt the contents of the cupboard almost before he had opened the door. The aroma from the grilling sausages made him swallow his saliva in yearning.

The plates were out on the table and Helen and Jetta had supper ready before Jetta spoke to Mat. He and Jake were talking about work when Jetta suddenly broke into the conversation.

"Look," she said, "is it not about time you were starting work again?"

Mat stood and looked at her. He had been thinking the same thing himself—his novel had got into such a mess that he couldn't envisage ever finishing it. He was about to agree with Jetta when something stopped him—in all the lines of her body Jetta stood there disapproving of him; even in Jake, as he stood there looking at him, he could feel the disappoval. There were all the things in them which would be left unsaid, but which were there—he had neglected Helen, subjected her to this life, and the baby. He was a layabout, a useless loafer, a lazy good-for-nothing. Even the supper they were about to eat, the cigarette he was smoking, were reproaches. He felt angry, but also he had a desperate need to justify himself. Sometimes he had asked himself why he did this—expose himself to every kind of humiliation and abuse. Not just from his own family, to all these strangers to whom he owed money, to these neighbours who sneered at him with their sly smiles because he wasn't working. He hated all this, hated and abominated it—that he should be dependent in any way on other people for anything. He had to cower and cringe and fawn when what he wanted to do was to spit in their eye. But this dependency—even this—he was enduring for the sake of something about which he was half-hearted and dubious. It seemed the only sensible thing to do, to start work again, yet even at this point he still wanted time. He didn't think it was worth it—yet he knew he couldn't stop. It was like a kind of tick in himself which he couldn't control. He opened his mouth to speak, sawing at the air with one hand, "You see—" he was going to try and explain himself, but Jetta interrupted him.

"Oh, don't start. You can twist things round until they mean anything. You just can't go on like this. It's disgraceful. Writing! You've nae time to think of things like that. You've got a wife and wean depending on ye."

"It's not that. Look, I'm quite agreeable. I'm going to start."

"I should think so. I should damn well think so. Agreeable? I should think you'd be agreeable. Do you realise that *food* has been brought into the house?"

Archie Hind (b. 1928)
The Dear Green Place, Hutchinson (1966)

. . . We were conducted . . . into a room where about twenty Scotch Drovers (i.e. cattle drivers) were regaling themselves with whisky and potatoes.

Robert Chambers
Walks in Edinburgh (1825)

Mid-day Meal ashore

We now agreed to camp after passing the little village of Ashton and partake of our first meal of the cruise.

This mid-day meal ashore is, next to evening repast in the tent, the most enjoyable event of the day—in fine weather—and somehow I rarely have had, in a thousand miles' cruising, to seek shelter at noon. Here is a sample of daily occurrence.

Hour, 1p.m.—Fix on some likely green patch, with a gentle slope, with the choicest scenery you can select full in view; see the spot be sheltered from the wind. Here spread the ground-sheet previously stowed handy for this purpose. Make another journey to the canoe, and, if that canoe be the *Severn*, you will find a certain hamper that just fits in beside the centre board. It is packed with the cuisine, a tin of cooked sausages, a small camp pie, fowl, tin of soup, or whatever of that ilk may have been selected for that day. Add to these a small tin of salt, a small bottle of pepper, knives and forks, some cooked fruit, honey, butter, and a mite of cheese, with a few similar etcæteras, and our daily fare is thus ready; its receptacle being known as "the lunch basket." The water bottle, pipe and tobacco pouch, are never left behind. Then the cuisine is started to boil the soup. Usually the first course is soup and bread, and the next will be meat and either bread or potatoes, which it is my habit to get cooked at a cottage hard by whenever possible. On more than one occasion I have had potatoes cooked and ready to eat under half-hour. Never, perhaps, has a potato a richer flavour than on such occasions. I have done this in Scotland (in former years); on the Severn, Thames, Avon, Wye, the Berkeley Canal, the Wear, and other waters, and I have found it infinitely better than wasting an hour or two in preparing and cooking them in the middle of the day. After meat of course we have fruit, or bread and butter with honey, and afterwards a little taste of cheese.

T. L. Holding
Watery Wanderings Mid Western Lochs
London: Malborough (1886)

Tom Hubbard

Variatioun on Ane Popular Theme

Aa o a sudden
A great mealie-pudden
Cam fleein throu the air:
Yin thocht it wis the verra bouk o Scotlan
The efterbirth o the warld's beginnin,
That wadna laund an rot, or the warld's end.
Anither wad hae
It wis nae mair nor a pudden
That had sae birkilie won free o the chip shop.

The first cheered it on:
Fair flochtie he wis, he fidgit in feerach at sic a fine ferlie;
The pudden tuik tent o this—its morale wis fair boostit —
An breengin on at fou dreel, it passed ayont lochans an
         knowes.
Its prood partisan wis pechin, he cuidna keep up wi 't,
An had ti gie owre,
Greetin wi joy
That he'd gien sic a heeze ti . . . weill, whitever it wis.

The saicont was thrawn.
He wad hae nane o't.
He shuik his pow (an his neive) as the pudden upby
Becam nae mair nor a peerie smitch i the lift.
He mairched richt up ti the first
An delivered himsel o his scunner,
Ti wit:
That there wis nae excaise fir the thing's behaviour;
Nae maitter whit kinna pudden it wis —
Reid, white or bleck —
It wis a bleck affront
Nae ti be tholed: they suid hae sent fir the polis.

Suppose it set ane precedent,
An its brithers up an cried:
'Suppers unite! Ye've naethin ti tyne but yer batters!'
Juist think o't—haddocks, fish-cakes, hamburgers, links
An even the tatties, the umwhile moderates —
Aa gangin camsteerie,
An formin a squadron o subversive sunkets
Ti follae thon pudden. An think o the effect
On the warld's air traffic, and, as the eftercast,
On business confidence. Aa governments
Wad siccarlie collapse.
                  —Sic whigmaleeries
Were nae fir the like o us, lat alane puddens!

The first chiel laucht.
He'd heard it aa afore.
He simplie gied a souch, as gin he wunnert
Gif the pudden wad, in time, come back ti him,
Bearin the gree:
Or (doolie thocht) gif it be dingit doun,
Ti lig an muilder i the wulderness.

Ignorin his wersh an fushionless companion
He laucht an grat in turn, an cried ti the lift:
'Whane'er sall I again behauld your face,
o my great chieftain o the pudden race?'

Tom Hubbard (b. 1950)
Four Fife Poets, AUP (1988)

David Hume

The Philosopher as Cook

Edinburgh 16 October 1769. . . . I have been settled here two Months, and am here Body & Soul, without casting the least Thought of Regreat to London, or even to Paris. I think it improbable that I shall ever in my Life cross the Tweed, except perhaps a Jaunt to the North of England, for Health or Amusement. I live still, and must for a twelvemonth, in my old House in James's Court, which is very chearful, and even elegant, but too small to display my great Talent for Cookery, the Science to which I intend to addict the remaining Years of my Life; I have just now lying on the Table before me a Receipt for making *Soupe a la Reine,* copy'd with my own hand. For Beef and Cabbage (a charming Dish), and old Mutton and old Claret, no body excels me. I make also Sheep head Broth in a manner that Mr Keith speaks of it for eight days after, and the Duc de Nivernois woud bind himself Apprentice to my Lass to learn it. I have already sent a Challenge to David Moncrief. You will see, that in a twelvemonth he will take to the writing of History, the field I have deserted: For as to the giving of Dinners, he can now have no farther Pretensions. I should have made a very bad use of my Abode in Paris, if I could not get the better of a mere provincial like him. All my Friends encourage me in this Ambition; as thinking it will rebound very much to my Honour.

I am delighted to see the daily and hourly Progress of Madness and Folly and Wickedness in England. The Consummation of these Qualities are the true Ingredients for making a fine Narrative in History; especially if followed by some signal and ruinous Convulsion, as I hope will soon be the Case with that pernicious People. He must be a very bad Cook indeed, that cannot make a palatable Dish from the whole. You see in my Reflections and Allusions I still mix my old and new Profession together.

I am Dear Sir Gilbert
Your most obedient Servant,
David Hume

David Hume (1711-76)
A Scottish Postbag
ed. George Bruce and Paul H. Scott, Edinburgh (1986)

Irn Bru and Square Slice

At my one visit to old-time Wembley, Scotland gave a 3-2 doing to the Saxons, who happened to be calling themselves world champions at the time. After taking a refreshment, I fell on to the top bunk of a train sleeper from Euston. At wakey-wakey time the mouth felt like the inside of Jim Baxter's stockings. Silently over the rim of the bed appeared a bottle of Irn Bru. With my provident companion from downstairs, who turned out to be a van driver and a Clyde supporter, there was a happy hour of living the triumph all over again, while we took our mornings of his Bru and what we could find in our half-bottles.

The nearer the train got to Glasgow, the more the early Sunday hours promised to be the start of another great day. Perfect happiness was being further improved with golden sunshine from an operatic blue sky. At the sight of the first corporation bus—looking lost and shy the way they all do from a train as if not sure of the way back to town—the wee man tidied his appearance with wetted fingers and made a check of the presents he had for his grandchildren. He readied away the remains of our picnic. He reckoned he still had left the price of his bus fare home to Bridgeton. Going over the river bridge, he remarked that that would be the wife getting up and putting the frying pan on. He said he could smell the square sausages and the black pudding already. Outside the station we shook hands goodbye.

Walking away round the camera shop corner, he paused and raised his arms above his head, his carrier bag dangling from a wrist, and did a wee jig to himself. His bantam figure embodied bliss. There was a man so adept at living his life that for a foreseen emergency he knew a way to keep by him a bottle of his favourite ginger for two nights and a day. He was a survivor. His little dance was when I began to see what it is to belong to Glasgow and for it to belong to you. Man and place were an exact fit. He was home where there is no better place.

William Hunter (b. 1931)
The Glasgow Herald Book of Glasgow, Mainstream (1989)

Alexander Hutchison

Surprise, Surprise

McSween the corner butcher with confidence displays
for denizens of the city—'of toons the *a per se*'—
a vegetarian haggis, rank of specimen of his craft.
Just what the creature might contain defeats surmise:
pinmeal and onions, nuts or beans, some dribs and drabs.
No gristle, no suet, no organ meats: no liver, no tripes
no light, no heart. Instead of a sheep's paunch
potato skins with a saddle-stitch fly. Up the Mound
down the Candlemakers Row the fix is in. The *makars* jump
the pebbles stump, the market splits wide open.

First *from a purely culinary point of view*—corned, curried
devilled, smoked and kosher haggis a la king; wee cocktail
haggis; haggis in a basket; haggis on the half shell; *instant* haggis;
English haggis; haggis eclairs; Crimean campaign haggis, conceived
in Sebastopol, consumed in Balaclava; hot-cross haggis; haggis in
plum sauce; desiccated haggis; baked haggis alaska; chocolate mint-
chip haggis; non-stick convenient haggis; cucumber and haggis
sandwiches; junk haggis; whole-hog haggis.

Next *by haggis of a special bent*—weight-watcher haggis;
haggis for the moonstruck; haggis *nouveau*; haggis *gran cru*; 12 year
old vintage haggis matured in oak casks; 100 year old Kung Po haggis
drawn from the well without obstruction; 'Bomber' haggis; haggis for
lovers; lite lo-tar, lo-nicotine haggis; Campdown haggis; drive-in
haggis; hand-raised, house-trained haggis, with pedigree attached;
haggis by special appointment; reconstituted haggis; nuclear-free
haggis; ancient Dynastic haggis sealed in canopic jars; haggis
quck step; haggis high in fibre; haggis low in the opinion of several
discerning people; a haggis of the Queen's flight; Nepalese temple
haggis (rich, dark and mildew-free); hard-porn haggis;
haggis built to last.

Finally *objects tending to the metaphysical*—desolation
haggis; the canny man's haggis; haggis not so good or bad as
one imagines; haggis made much of caught young; unsung haggis;
haggis not of this fold; haggis dimm'd by superstition;
perfectly intuited haggis; haggis beyond the shadow of a doubt;
bantering haggis; haggis given up for Lent; haggis given up for
lost; haggis so good you think you died and went to heaven;
haggis supreme; haggis unchained.

Alexander Hutchison (b. 1944)
The Moon Calf, Galliard (1990)

But now the Supper crowns their simple board,
The healsome Porritch, chief of SCOTIA's food:
The soup their only Hawkie does afford,
That 'yont the hallan snugly chows her cood:
The Dame brings forth, in complimental mood,
To grace the lad, her weel-hain'd kebbuck, fell,
And aft he's prest, aft he ca's it guid;
The frugal Wifie, garrulous, will tell,
How 'twas a towmond auld, sin' Lint was i' the bell.

Robert Burns (1759-96)
'The Cotter's Saturday Night'
Poems (1786)

The Snapdragon

This story came from my late mother's aunt, but I'm afraid we don't know and can't find out where she got it from (whether a book or journal). But it would have been published somewhere, as there is an Irish version in a book by Somerville and Ross. We think, however, that the Scots version is the original, and comes from the North East, occuring towards the end of the last century. Unfortunately none of us seem to know it by heart so I'm afraid I have had to improvise in places.

Efter the Blessing was ca'ed, there was set doon afore me a fine slab o' beef, biled, wi' the fat attached, and, forbye, a hale moontain o'carrots, tatties and the like. Syne, the Laird addressed a remark tae me, so I set doon ma knife and ma fork, decent-like, tae gi'e ma reply. I hadnae done speaking when by cam' a slotch o' a lad, and snappit up ma plate, oot o' ma sicht.

Files, the Laird, seeing I had nae fuid, speirt—had they nae brocht ma helping? "It's here and awa', Laird!" I said; so he ca'ed for't, and it was set afore me: a slab o' beef, biled, and wi' the fat attached, and a fair heap o' carrots, tatties and the like. So I set masel' to it but nae for lang, since the Laird addressed a remark tae me:—"Fit like was ma hairst?" So I set doon ma knife and ma fork, decent-like, tae gi'e ma reply, and by come yon creepin' snapdragon, and snappit up ma plate, oot o' ma sicht.

Syne, the Laird speirt me, "Have they no' brocht yer fuid *yet*, Birsebeg".

"It was 'Come and go', Sir!" I said til'm. So he ca'ed for't, and it was set afore me: a slab o' beef, biled, and wi' the fat attached, and a puckle o' carrots, tatties and the like. Syne, the Laird speirt me; "Fit like are yer neaps, Birsebeg?" So I set doon ma knife, but retained me fork, for I spied yon creepin' slotch o' a snapdragon skulkin' in the shadows. "Ye'll no' hae't this time, ye rascal!", I thocht, and when his haun' cam' raxin' for ma plate, I turned, sudden-like, wi' the fork up-raised, and cried on'm,

"Dinnae you tak' it awa', ye snapdragon, or I'll staup ye tae the vitals!"

Rosemary Innes
(written for this book)

Breakfast

Not long after the dram, may be expected the breakfast, a meal in which the Scots, whether of the lowlands or mountains, must be confessed to excel us. The tea and coffee are accompanied not only with butter, but with honey, conserves, and marmalades. If an epicure could remove by a wish, in quest of sensual gratifications, wherever he had supped he would breakfast in Scotland.

Samuel Johnson (1709-1784)
Journey to the Western Islands of Scotland, London (1775)

For breakfast . . . the cheese was set out as before, with plenty of butter and barley cakes, and fresh oaten cakes, which no doubt were made for us: they were kneaded with cream and were excellent.

Dorothy Wordsworth
Recollections of a Tour made in Scotland (1803)

I Try my Absolute Best

I give my kids pure apple juice
(no sugar less acid than orange)
buy my baby soya milk formula
now she's off the breast
(non dairy, no cholesterol, good
for their little hearts—apparently
their arteries can harden before five
even). Water from the purifier.
Perrier if I'm feeling flush,
(they can always pretend that it's lemonade).
Carob coated date bars. Cherry or banana.
And there's a shop down the street
that is selling organic vegetables
(no sprays, no chemicals).
Only to find the bloody English apples
are being sprayed with alar and are
carcinogenic; the soya beans are cooked
in aluminium pots which gives off deposits
in the brain; the cartridge in the purifier
collects things (like knickers if they're not changed).
Perrier's got Benzene in it which gives rats
cancer. Though I personally don't know any rat
that drinks Perrier, do you? And them
so-called Health Food Bars contain more sugar
than the average Mars Bar. What's the use
in calling anything organic when
the bloody soil's chock-a-block with lead?

I try my absolute best
drink decaff coffee to pipe me down
instead of hype me up only to find
out from my eldest daughter
that what they put the beans through
is worse for you than an ordinary Nescafe.

I'm back on Valium.
My kids are stuffing Monster Munch
and Mars Bars down them.

My youngest son even ate a hamburger yesterday.
It's driving me crazy.
I says it's your pocket money,
Do what you want with it.

Jackie Kay (b. 1961)
The Adoption Papers, Bloodaxe (1991)

"Dinna let me catch ye stravaygin' awa' again, or ye'll get nae
carvies tae yer tea."

J.J.Bell (1871-1934)
Wee Macgregor (1902)

James Kelman

Monday is Mince and Potatoes

3/4lb beef links, 1lb of potatoes, 2 onions medium sized and 1 tin beans
baked. And that's you with the sausage, chips and beans plus the juicy
onions—and they're good for your blood whether you like it or no. This
big pot with this grill type container is for the chips, it lets them drip so
the fat goes back into the pot. Simple economics. And even if your
mummy's sick to death of chips, what should be said is this: she isnt the
fucking cook the day so enough said, let her go to a bastarn cafe. 2
nights on the trot is okay as long as it's not regularly the case. Fine: the
items should get dished no more than 4 times per week but attempt to
space it so that 1 day can pass without. 7 days in a week. What is that by
christ is there an extra day floating about somewhere? Best to ignore
fixed things like weeks and months and the rest of it. That's the time
thing they set you up. Just think of the days. The minimum to cover all of
the things i.e. breakfast, dinner, tea. Right: chips number 1 day, 3 day, 5
day, 7 day; missing 0 day, 2 day, 4 day and 6 day. Alright, 8 times a fortnight.
But 7 every 14 days. So there you are you can maybe get left having
them twice on the trot but being a chip lover you just ignore it. Let's go
then: right; Monday is fish day—rubbish. Monday is mince and potatoes.
Simple, get your pot. Item: 1 pot: 3/4 lb mince. Item: 2 onions medium
sized, then a 1/2 lb carrots, a tin of peas and also a no—not at all, dont
use a frying pan to brown the mince; what you do is fry it lightly in the
same pot you're doing the actual cooking in. Saves a utensil for the
cleaning up carry on. So: stick mince into pot with drop cooking oil, lard
or whatever the fuck—margarine maybe. Have onions peeled and
chopped. Break up mince with wooden spoon. Put pot on at slow heat
that it doesnt sizzle too much. While breaking up mince all the time in
order that it may not become too fucking lumpy. Toss in onions. The
pepper and salt to have been sprinkled while doing the breaking up.
Next: have your water boiled. Pour a 1/2 pint measure in which you've
already dumped gravy cube viz crumbled into the smallest bits possible.
Stir. When mince brownish add mixture. Stir. Place lid on pot. Having
already brought to boil. Then get simmering i.e. once boiling you turn
gas so's it just bubbles and no more. Pardon. Once you've got 1/2 pint
gravy water poured in you'll probably need extra. Lid on. Handle turned

to inside lest accidents to person. Then sit on arse for following hour apart from occasional checks and stirring. 30 minutes before completion you get the spuds peeled and cut into appropriate sections and fill the other pot with boiling water, having already dumped said spuds into pot while empty for fuck sake otherwise you'll splash yourself. Stick on at hot heat. Sit on arse for 15 to 20 minutes. Open tin peas of course. The bastarn fucking carrots. At the frying mince and onion stage you've got them peeled and chopped and you add to same. The peas get placed in wee saucepan and can cook in matter of moments. When time's up you've got mince, potatoes and peas set to serve from trio of pots.

James Kelman (b. 1946)
The Busconductor Hines, Polygon (1984)

Stovies

One and a half pounds of Mutton
One pound of Potatoes
Pepper and Salt
One Onion
Half a small Turnip
One tablespoonful of Suet

METHOD:
Cut mutton up finely; chop suet; put these in pan and pour on enough boiling waster to cover; simmer gently for one hour. Chop onion finely, cut potato and turnip up roughly, and add these and stew gently for another hour; season and serve hot.

Tea and Biscuits

I always seem to think of Michael in the kitchen. He is at his clearest then, perhaps because we were busy together there, visiting each other, interrupting, letting things boil. I can smell the wet earth from the potatoes, our red, clay soil. He takes oranges and orange scent from a brown paper bag.

"Fifty pence for five. That's not bad. They're big."

"You're mean, you know that? I've noticed."

"They're big oranges, look. I'm not mean."

"You're stingy."

"Nice, cheap oranges. I am not stingy."

"You're a stingy, grouchy, old man."

He was wearing the big coat, the blue one. It smelt of evening weather and the car. I slipped my arms inside it and around his waist. That was something I did a lot.

"You're just after my oranges."

"That's right."

Michael stood very still for a while. He said,

"You do make me happy sometimes. You don't know."

The dinner was good, with oranges after.

If I'd come to the park last week the afternoon would have been longer, but evenings come in fast now. You can see the change from day to day. By the time I get home the lights will be in the windows and Michael will be back, the fires on. He doesn't like the house to be cold.

I will tell him then. I think I will tell him.

I went there because it's a public service. In the student days we came for the tea and biscuits, but it felt good afterwards, just the same. You knew you could have saved a life. You hadn't run into a burning building or pulled a child out of the sea, but part of you had been taken and it would help someone. I liked it when they laid you on your bed with so many other people, all on their beds, all together with something slightly nervous and peaceful in the air.

They would talk to you and find a vein, do it all so gently, and I would ask for the bag to hold as it filled. The nurse would rest it on my stomach and I would feel the weight in it growing and the strange warmth. It was a lovely colour too. A rich, rich red. I told my mother about it and she laughed.

I gave them my blood a couple of times after that, then my periods made me anaemic and then I forgot. I don't know what made me start to go back.

Nothing much had changed, only the form at the beginning which was different and longer and I lay on a bed in a bus near the shopping centre, not in a thin, wooden hall.

Afterwards they send you a certificate. It comes in the post and you get a little book to save them in, like co-op stamps. This time they sent me a letter instead. It was a kind, frightening letter which said I should come and see someone; there might be something wrong with my blood.

I am full of blood. My heart is there for moving blood. The pink under my fingernails is blood. I can't take it away.

And now I am not what I thought I was. I am waiting to happen. I have a clock now, they told me that. A drunk who no longer drinks is sober, but he has a clock because every new day might be the day that he slips. His past becomes his achievement, not his future. I have a clock like that. I look at my life backwards and all of it's winding down. I think that is how it will stay. I think that's it.

Should I say it to Michael like that? Should I tell him that thing I remember about the American tribe. Those Indians. They thought that we went through life on a river, all facing the stern of the boat and we only ever looked ahead in dreams. That's what I'll have to do now.

I think he told me about that. It sounds like him. It would give us some kind of start for the conversation.

A. L. Kennedy (b. 1965)
Night Geometry and the Garscadden Trains, Polygon (1990)

Alison Kermack

A Wee Tatty

He goat the idea offy the telly. Heard oan the news this Chinese boy hud ritten 2000 characters oan a singul grainy rice. Well o coarse, he kidny rite Chinese and he dooted if thur wiz any rice i the hoose (unless mebby in the chinky cartons fi last nite). Butty liked the idea. Whit wi the asbestos fi wurk damajin his lungs an him oan the invalidity an that. Well. He hudda loatty time tay himsel an no much munny ti day anyhin wi it. Anny didny reckon he hud long tay go noo. It wid be nice, yi ken, jist tay day sumhin tay leeve sumhin behind that peepul wid mebby notice. Jist a wee thing.

So wunce the bairnz wur offty skule an the wife wiz offty wurk, he cleared the kitchin table an hud a luke in the cubburds. Rite enuff, nay rice. He foond sum tattys but. Thottyd better scrub thum furst so he did. Then took thum back tay the table. He picked the smollist wun soze it wizny like he wiz cheatin too much, anny began tay rite oan it wi a byro.

He stied ther aw day. Kept on gawn, rackiniz brains an straynin tay keepiz hand fi shaykin. Efter 7 oors o solid con-sen-tray-shun, he ran ooty space. Heed manijd tay rite 258 swayr wurds oan the wee tatty. He sat back tay huv a luke. Even tho heed scrubd it, it wiz still a bit durty-lukin an it wiz that fully ize yi kidny see the rytin very well. But still. He felt heed acheeved sumhin. He wiz fuckn nackert. He laydiz heed doon oan the table an fella sleep. He didny wake up.

When his wife goat back fi hur wurk, she foond the boady lyin it the table. She gret a wee bit but theyd bin expectin it. She pickt him up an, strugglin under the wait, tryd tay shiftim inty the back bedroom. Haff way throo it goat tay much furrur an she hud tay leevim in the loabby til she goat a naybur tay helpur.

Wunce she goatim throo the back, she sat doon it the table an thot aboot how tay tell the bairnz. Mebby efter thur tea. Aw kryst, haff foar, she better pit the tea oan. Thursday so thur wizny much in the hoose. She noticed the tattys oan the table an thot it wiz nice o hur man tay scrub thum furrur. She chopped thum up an pit thum oan tay bile.

That nite, even tho the bairnz didny notice, the tiny drop o ink made the stovyz tayst that wee bit diffrint.

Alison Kermack *Original Prints 4*, Polygon (1992)

Table Manners

"I can't find no bottom to your hunger," Matron had said of them, anxious, puzzled as if the fault was her own. "There never seems to be enough for you."

'Table manners' which they had to memorise in their first weeks in the orphanage had no 'small print' as warning!

> In silence I must take my seat
> and say my Grace before I eat
> Must for my food with patience wait
> Till I am asked to hand my plate
> Must turn my head to cough or sneeze
> And when I ask, say 'if you please'.
> I must not speak a useless word
> For children should be seen not heard
> I must not talk about my food
> Nor fret if I don't think it good.
> My mouth with food I must not crowd
> Nor while I'm eating speak aloud.
> When told to rise then I must put
> My chair away with noiseless foot
> and lift my heart to God above
> In praise for all His wondrous love

It never mentioned porridge! Nor the fact that if you didn't eat your porridge you got no tea and bread and butter to follow.

Orphanage porridge, made the night before, so that by morning you could cut it up into thick, lukewarm slices, sent even Chris's voracious, indiscriminate stomach rising up in revolt. James Dobie became her eager and willing receptacle. Thus, the pact was formed. Wolfing down his own portion, while Chris picked warily round the edge of her plate. The transference of plates, with years of practice behind it, was a miracle of dexterity and timing.

Jessie Kesson (1916-94)
Where the Apple Ripens, Hogarth Press (1985)

The Royal Salmon

Queen Victoria's command for 'A simple picnic hamper, plus kitchen maids.' from Balmoral Castle signified informal living at her 'Widow's House' in Glen Muick. But when the other diners refused Faro's attempts at polite conversation, his worst fears were justified.

Obviously the Royal rule of 'half-an-hour only for all meals' was still in force. Her Majesty gobbled her food at an alarming rate, her soup plate emptied, bread demolished before the diners had taken more than two spoonsful.

At Inspector Faro's side the Captain of the Household Guard belched loudly. "Beg pardon, sir. Indigestion, y'know. Absolute hell. Now you understand why." And as Faro commiserated with him, the salmon course hove into view.

"Don't waste time talking to me, sir, I beg you," the Captain interposed, already brandishing knife and fork. "Just keep eating, or you'll be starving by morning."

The Royal Salmon was the Inspector's particular favourite. He had been particularly relishing this course, especially since he had narrowly escaped death at the hands of an unseen assassin during the catching of it that afternoon. Now he managed only a few forksful before that plate too was whipped away. Resentfully he saw that the Queen was drumming her fingers on the tablecloth, impatiently awaiting her own particular favourite, Scotch Trifle.

Alanna Knight
To Kill a Queen, Macmillan (1992)

Recipes for:

INSPECTOR FARO'S ROYAL SALMON

Individual fillets of fresh salmon, rolled in lightly salted plain flour, dipped in beaten egg and then covered in porridge oats. In Queen Victoria's kitchens at Balmoral, these were spread with butter and baked in a hot oven. For today's diners, grill for about 8 mins or until salmon is thoroughly cooked (depending on thickness of fillets). Serve with buttered carrots, broccoli and creamed potatoes.

and
SCOTCH TRIFLE; THE ROYAL FAVOURITE

Plain sponge cake, 1 pint Custard, 1 schooner Sherry, raspberry jelly; small tin of fruit (peaches, apricots, or cocktail assortment); 1/2 pint double cream.

Soak sponge in sherry; Make up jelly to three-quarters pint, add fruit juice, pour over sponge. allow to set; add fruit, and thick custard. Add whipped cream before serving.

The Appetite

That conversation was a tread,
a trampoline. 'Words are absurd',
it said, and our eyes played
at not being on it, laughing.

We sat facing each other, eating
as if
we sat facing each other, eating.

Tom Leonard (b. 1944)
Intimate voices
Galloping Dog Press (1984)

Maurice Lindsay

Breakfast at Sea

My school chum, Granville Ramage, a classical scholar who later became a diplomat, had his home in Orkney, his father being parish minister on the island of Stronsay. During the late summers of the thirties, I spent the month of July with the Ramages in Orkney and Granville spent August with the Lindsays at Innellan. I felt strongly drawn to the long clear summer light that lies across the Orkney Islands. . . .

The island of Stronsay was then still a thriving herring port, out of which sailed a sizeable fleet of steam drifters during the summer season. One night we wangled ourselves a trip to the fishing grounds aboard an ancient steam drifter, the *Christmas Morn*. The sail far into the North Sea, on a night near enough the back of mid-summer for darkness to be little more than a few hours of smudged charcoal against a smoulder of deep gold, ended in what seemed to us simply a stretch of edgeless sea, but to the fishermen meant the presence of a possible catch. Distant on the horizon were the faint little silhouettes of other drifters, rolling, no doubt, on the unbroken swell as gently as the *Christmas Morn*. Slowly the nets were tumbled out behinds us; then we settled down patiently to wait. Crouched uncomfortably in the wheelhouse we dozed uneasily, the phosphorescent sea glinting around us and softly slapping the vessel's hull.

Suddenly it was uncramping morning, a cold breeze rising, machinery revolving, orders shouting. As the nets were hauled back over the stern the sea gasped out its silver harvest, the herring slithering and twitching over the rim of the hold, or flapping about on the deck, speckled now and then with a crimson splash where the toy-shark teeth of a dog-fish had sunk in and severed. Dog-fish that tangled the net, or lay thumping the deck, were unceremoniously flung back into the sea, their heads first being knocked against the gunnels. On the way home, the smell of oil from the engines and the gritty smoke from the funnels mingled with the aroma of freshly frying herring, a hungry breakfast with a singular edge of appetite.

Maurice Lindsay (b. 1920)
Thank You for Having Me, Hale (1983)

Robert Lindsay

The Earl of Atholl
Entertains James V

[The] palice withtin was weill syllit and hung witht fyne tapistrie and arrasis of silk, and sett and lightit witht glassin wondowis in all airttis [so] that this palice was allis pleisantlie decoirit witht all necessaris pertenand to ane prince as it had bene his awin palice royall at hame. Farder this earle gart mak sic provitioun ffor the king and his mother and that stranger the ambassadour that thai had all maner of meittis, drinkis, deliecattis that was to be gottin at that tyme in al Scottland either in burght or in land that might be gottin for money; that is to say, all kynd of drink, as aill, beir, wyne, batht quhyte wyne and clairit, mallvesie musticat and allacant, inchethrist and accqquitie. Ffarder thair was of meittis, of breid quhyte breid maine breid and gingebreid, witht flesches, beif, muttun, lambes, cuning, cran, suan, wile guse, pertrick and plever, duke, Brissill cok and powins togither witht blak cok and murefoull and cappercallzes; and also the stankis that was round about the palice was sowmond full of all deliecat fisches, as sallmond, troutis and perches, pykis and eilis and all wther kynd of deliecat fisches that could be gottin in fresche watteris was all redy to be prepairit for the bancat. Syne was thair proper stewartis and cuning baxteris and also excellent cuikis and potiseris witht confectiounis and drogis ffor thair desairtis. All thir thingis beand in order and prepairit as I haue schawin, hallis, chameris and witht costlie beding, weschell and naiperie according for ane king, nathing deminischit of this ordour more nor he had bene at hame in his awin palice.

Robert Lindsay of Pitscottie (c. 1532-90)
Historie and Cronikles of Scotland (c. 1575)
Scottish Text Society, (1899-1911)

In 1530 the Earl or Atholl built a "Curious Palace" of wood to entertain James V (1512–42) and the Papal Ambassador after a hunting party in the Highlands.

Mull Broth

Michael got the stove going for the soup. Between us we had one tin of vegetable soup and one of oxtail. Mull Broth, we named it. The pan was was still generously endowed with this morning's porridge—all part of the famous recipe, we decided. Whilst gathering firewood under the trees I found a mushroom. Into the broth it went . . . as did a crumbling and sodden heap that had once been a packet of biscuits. The hoods of our anoraks were up for protection, not from the rain but from dark clouds of midges. We huddled over a sulky, smoky fire which did nothing to dry the clothes festooning the branches above, but at least kept the tormenting swarms at bay while we drank our broth.

"Special protein-enriched broth," Michael said as he stirred in a score or more of midges who had volunteered themselves as an addition to the recipe.

Robin Lloyd-Jones (b. 1934)
Argonauts of the Western Isles
Diadem Books (1989)

Cocky Leeky is a soup made of fowl with leeks, to which an alliance with a piece of beef is very advisable; the leeks are very little shorn, so as to make it difficult to eat it without offence against delicacy by some slobbering. I remember an English gentleman who was mentioning a dinner he had got in Edinburgh in which tho' the soup was excellent he could not recollet its name. "But it was a soup," said he, "of which a mouthful was one half in the mouth and the other half out."

Henry Mackenzie (1745-1831)
Anecdotes and Egotisms (1927)

Liz Lochhead

Mrs Abernethy: Festive Fayre

(MONOLOGUE)

Well . . . *wait* till I tell you. It was not Christmas for me this Christmas. Telling you Christmas dinner's no picnic for The Lady of the House at the best of times and this year was no exception. I just said to my hubby this morning, I said, "The sooner its the Sixth of January and we've got a they decorations back up the loft and poked all they clogged-up pine needles out the Hoover tube with a knitting needle and its back to auld claes and parritch the better pleased I'll be."

Honestly its been bake, bake, bake. The beaters of my Kenwood have seldom been still since the end of November. Between the Cubs Christmas Fayre and the Girls Guildry conversazzione, and I'd two dozen melting moments for the Brownies Bring and Buy. Still it was appreciated and thats the main thing. Brown Owl said to me your melting moments go like snow aff a dyke. Still it'll be with folk knowing where they came from. Our Gillian got terrible food poisoning off strange tablet at a Garden Fete once.

Och but don't mention our Gillian to me. Its her that I'm vexed at. That girl ruined Christmas for the whole family. Well, its a busy time for her da as well, what with those extra services—and a lamentable feature of this day and age is the amount of toerags that roll in bold as brass to the Watchnight Service *reeking* of drink.

Well, Gillian's always been very independent. Well we've *encouraged* that. We've encouraged that. My Better Half's always maintained, and I agree with him, if they don't want to go to the Church then we won't force them. After all one of the dogmas of the Protestant faith has always been a freedom of choice. I mean John Knox and Martin Luther Thingmy, I mean they built the Kirk on the tenets of independence. I mean I'm no historian, you'd have to check up on this with my hubby, but as far as I know the Reformation started up North in Europe a guid lang mile away from Rome and the Pope and that, up in the Region of what we now know as Holland, and Germany and Alsace Lorraine. In fact, correct me if I'm wrong, but I think that Protestantism was originally an Alsatian Dogma.

So they've not been regular attenders since the age of fourteen or so and their dad and me have always been very tolerant. And Valerie, that's the elder girl, has been a model daughter in every other way. Five Highers, Jordanhill, married in the University Chapel to an awful nice electrical engineer who wouldn't say boo, taught for two years till she got her parchment before starting a family. And wee Kate and Joshua are just plain gorgeous even though it's their Granny talking. Valerie's got some wee 'do' on tonight and I popped over to Hyndland Road this morning because she was short of ramekins for her starters and the wee souls were all over Gran with their Selection Boxes, honestly any more would sicken me.

But that Gillian. . . . Well, she phones me up to say could she bring a friend home for Christmas, I says you know your friends are always welcome, you don't have to ask. So she says Michael and I will be off the six fifteen at Central on the twenty third. Michael. Well, I thought nothing of it, because she's always palled up with a lot of English chaps since she was up at St Andrews and there was the odd Michael among them. Simon and Timothy and what not. Dampt few Alastairs and Kenneths anyway!

So, to cut a long story short, she arrives with this . . . Michael. And he seems very nice. Turns out his Dad is a head master in the Bathgate area so I says, Oh what's the school called? All innocence. St Francis Xavier says he without turning a hair. I didn't know where to look, and that bisum just sat there cool as a cucumber wolfing down my Celebration Chile con Carne Surprise. I mean, as I said to my hubby later on, we didn't scrimp and scrape to send her to Hutchy Girls so she would grow up to give us grandweans saying merr, flerr and sterr.

Still, it's her life to ruin and one word from us and she'll do the opposite so good luck to her, I wash my hands I wash my hands absolutely.

And now there's the Ne'erday to get by. I'll better away and get my black bun out the oven. I don't like to blow my own trumpet but My Better Half could eat it to a band playing. I like it, I *like* it alright, but does it like me, that's the trouble! At least I've my shortbread baked, I wouldn't give the bought stuff houseroom. Willie Learmouth the session clerk came by today for the Intimations and he's an awful nice man, one of Nature's Gentlemen, went to Allan Glen's when that *meant* something, his wife's got a plastic hip but you never hear him complain, anyway he sat down to a wee cup of tea and naturally he could not resist my all butter shortbread. "Nettie," says he "your petticoat tails would melt in a man's mouth."

Mibbe another batch wouldn't go wrong? Happy New Year everybody, although it'll be no holiday for me.

Liz Lochhead (b. 1947)
True Confessions and New Clichés
Polygon (1985)

A huge pot hung over the fire which leapt in a shining black-and-steel range. A black kettle stood on one hob, a brown teapot on the other. Steam rose gently from the kettle and thickly from the great back pot. Whence also came a continuous 'purring' noise and the wonderful smell.

Jennifer Gown
'Friendship is a Clootie Dumpling' *Scottish Field* (July 1966)

Brian McCabe

Hero Dumpling

Make way for the Dumpling, the Hero
Of a kitchen's Scottish history at last.
Let us celebrate the Hero Dumpling,
Rolled through two world wars to feed us.
Mummified in muslins, hung in cloutties.
Boiled for years in Brilloed jeely-pans
And swathed in a fat ghost of steam.
Sedater of the nation, the Dumpling
Has weighed upon the bellies of kings
And beggars alike, and will again!
Rich with the sweet, ancient raisins
Of our great-great-grannies' eyes.
Studded with our great-great-grandads'
Hard brass threepenny-bit teeth.
Here he comes, here comes the Hero:
This colossal arse of a pudding.
Like a monster's benappied bairn.
Solid as a medicine-ball, but riddled
With everyday riches: the fat
Of any ox's kidney's this poulticed
Bomb of spice and sweat and suet
Will keep for weeks, months, years —
It will last a lifetime of thrift
Wrapped in greaseproof and lardered.
Taken out to be sliced and fried.
Here is the Hero Dumpling at last:
So slap the Hero, slap him hard —
Give the Hero's arse a good hard slap.

Brian McCabe (b. 1951)
(previously unpublished)

Uncle Roderick

His drifter swung in the night
from a mile of nets
between the Shiants and Harris.

My boy's eyes watched
the lights of the fishing fleet—fireflies
on the green field of the sea.

In the foc's'le he gave me a bowl
of tea, black, strong and bitter
and a biscuit you hammered
in bits like a plate.

The fiery curtain came up
from the blackness, comma'd with corpses.

Round Rhu nan Cuideagan
he steered for home, a boy's god
in seaboots. He found his anchorage
as a bird its nest.

In the kitchen he dropped
his oilskins where he stood.

He was strong as the red bull.
He moved like a dancer.
He was a cran of songs.

Norman MacCaig (1910–96)
Collected Poems
Chatto and Windus, The Hogarth Press (1985)

Apricot Slice
in the People's Palace

it's raining cats and dogs
it's queuing pensioners
it's pizzicato on the roof
it's tea and apricot slice and a smile
carried joyfully to a damp bench
under palms that ambush me
with inflated raindrops

it's you arriving, damp and scattered
and me with my cup filled to overflowing and
I press you to an apricot slice
a slab of orange happiness
and tart delight

we share a bench like two pigeons in winter
and watch an old man drawing

and a wedding party enters, pink and white
with sober suits and cameras
for photos among ferns, and palms, in Paradise

paradise palms, the Winter Gardens
tasting of apricots, and you beside me
a palace in Glasgow in the rain

Mary McCann
Scream, if you want to go faster
New Writing Scotland 9, ASLS (1991)

I am Very Fond of Grub

Orlando's punch, Granny's soup and cans of beer, sandwiches, sausages and potato crisps. This was where Geordie Anderson first appeared. No one knew who brought him, but some had seen him before, with his Jolson make-up.

"God love him," said Granny. "He could be wan o yer ain."

"If you kid on you're daft you'll get a hurl for nothing," said Orlando.

At some point Geordie would stand to sing, would carry on with songs of his own devising until told to sit down, whereupon he sat down immediately and waited for another opportunity to stand up and sing until told to stop.

> I am very fond of grub, grub is very nice,
> I like bacon, I like chips and I like bread and rice;
> There's lots and lots of stuff to eat, there's soup and
>   meat and stew,
> And if you've got a minute I will name them all to you:
> There's peas and beans, potatoes
> Sausages and ham
> Cornflakes and porridge
> Marmalade and jam;
> Trifle, tripe and a wee pig's feet,
> Chicken, eggs and chops;
> Fruit comes from the greengrocer
> And the meat from a butcher's shop. Oy.

'Geordie, sit doon.' 'Aye, that's enough Geordie; gie's peace.' The punch atmosphere poised on the edge of recklessness. There were a few bletherings which could have developed into argument, a series of breenges which could have become a fight. No one wanted soup or sandwiches and when Geordie stood up to sing again, he was shouted down.

Carl MacDougall (b. 1941)
The lights below, Secker & Warburg (1993)

The Butchers of Glasgow

The butchers of Glasgow have all got their pride
But they'll tell you that Willie's the prince
For Willie the butcher he slaughtered his wife
And he sold her for mutton and mince

It's a terrible story to have to be telt
And a terrible thing to be done
For what kind of man is it slaughters his wife
And sells her a shilling a pun

For lifting his knife and ending her life
And hanging her high like a sheep
You widnae object but you widnae expect
He wid sell the poor woman so cheap

But the Gallowgate folk were delighted
It didnae cause them any tears
They swore that Willie's wife Mary
Was the best meat he'd sold them for years

Matt McGinn (1928-77)
McGinn of the Calton, Glasgow City Libraries (1987)

Suzanna MacIver

A Good Scotch Haggies

Make the haggies-bag perfectly clean; parboil the draught; boil the liver very well, so as it will grate; dry the meal before the fire; mince the draught and a pretty large piece of beef very small; mix all these materials very well together, with a handful or two of the dried meal; spread them on the table, and season them properly with salt and mixed spices; take any of the scraps of beef that is left from mincing, and some of the water that boiled the draught, and make about a choppin of good stock of it: then put all the haggies-meat into the bag, and that broath in it: then sew up the bag; but be sure to put out all the wind before you sew it quite close. If you think the bag is thin, you may put it in a cloth. If it is large haggies, it will take at least two hours boiling.

Suzanna MacIver,
*Cookery and pastry. As taught and practised by Mrs MacIver,
teacher of those arts in Edinburgh, (1773).*

Lunch

The Cafe, long and narrow, was packed as usual. The three girls pushed past the wee ones at the sweetie counter to the hot-pie stand. The place was badly lit, but warm and smelling of cooked food. Downstairs, they could see workmen sitting at tables spooning soup into wide mouths. The owner gave them a big smile. He was a tall, immaculately-groomed, middle-aged man, ludicrously out of place.

"What can I do for you, Ladies?" he said, over the heads of two boys.

Kirsty's large breasts and swollen lips were an advantage wherever they went.

"Three hot pies," said Kirsty and fluttered her eyelids. He tried to serve the pies into paper bags without taking his eyes off Kirsty's front. He was improving, but his confidence was in advance of his technique. He let the last one fall on the counter.

"I'll give you half-price for that one," sneered Annie.

Being so thin, she looked three years younger than her friends. He ignored her, slipping the pie into a bag and pushing them across the counter towards the girls.

"Anything else, Ladies?" he smiled at Kirsty.

"I'm needing two fags," said Eileen quietly.

"I'll have the same," said Annie.

He reached behind him for a ten-packet lying open on the shelf and laid four cigarettes on the counter.

"And you, my dearie?" he smiled into Kirsty's eyes.

She cast them demurely down

"I'll have a doughring, pleath," she lisped.

Annie grinned round at Eileen, who was concentrating on easing the cigarettes into her top pocket. She watched the doughring being handed over.

"Greedy bitch," she thought.

They paid and left.

There was brief jockeying for position as they moved off. The one in the middle got better protection from the wind and Kirsty, the heaviest, usually landed there. They walked with elbows crammed against their ribs, both hands holding the hot pie. They passed two women teachers on their way to a restaurant lunch. In warms coats, they appeared little affected by the cold. Eileen and Kirsty pointedly looked away as the teachers passed, but Annie caught the eye of one of them and nodded.

They headed past the school and round to the graveyard. It was the oldest in town, with ancient gravestones rubbed smoothly illegible. Large, gnarled trees drooped over sections of it, creating bowers and semi-private areas used by couples and exhausted old folk in the summer. Now, with the trees stripped bare, human forms could be made out here and there.

The girls trudged to the centre area which, because of the lay-out of the paths and crush of gravestones, afforded the best concealment. Eileen and Kirsty sat down on a horizontal gravestone turned moss-green with age. Anne leaned against a nearby upright, preferring shelter to a seat. She scooped the pie out of the bag, wrapping it around with the paper. She concentrated her attention on it, shutting out all other impressions. Her tongue swimming in saliva, she took a deep bite and closed her eyes. She suppressed an image of Eileen eating, strands of hair in amongst her pie, and opened her eyes to the view.

She like the sombre greys and dark earth of the place, preferring now to the summer, when the leaf-slanted sunlight irritated her. The location of the graveyard acted as a wind tunnel and sun-bathing was better elsewhere. She closed her eyes and bit deep again. She could feel a trickle of grease ease itself from the corner of her mouth and she wiped it on the edge of the bag. She looked at the pie. Two more bites and it would be gone. Her toes were so cold that they were aching. Eileen's eyes were two black patches on a blue background, her lips mauve. Kirsty's face seemed to shrink with cold, her skin pulling taut. Her lips grew and her eyes bulged under a heavy, dark fringe.

Kirsty finished her pie and tossed the crumpled bag down, feeling for her cigarette packet. Annie took the last bite of her pie and began to smile. She waited until Kirsty's packet was open, then produced her matches.

"Light?" she said.

She stepped forward, twisting her head to see.

"Got enough, have you?" she said.

Kirsty flattened the packet against her chest and glared. Annie hadn't managed to see how many there were, but beamed at Kirsty.

"I'm fine, ta," said Kirsty and put a cigarette in her mouth. Annie waited for Eileen, then struck a match, cupping a hand round it. Eileen was too quick and knocked it out. Kirsty snatched the matches.

"Let me."

The wind took the first, but she lit up with the second, leaving two unspent.

"Anybody else got spunks?"

No-one answered. Eileen and Annie lit theirs off Kirsty's and Annie returned to her gravestone. She smiled at the whole cigarette in her hand.

"Ah'm gan back efter this. It's ower bloody al'," said Eileen. Kirsty brought out the doughring and took a big bite, eyes wide. Annie watched her, becoming aware that she was wearing an odd expression. She wasn't chewing properly, seeming to have difficulty with the lump in her mouth. Eileen was staring straight ahead, blankly. Annie turned her head to see, then heard the growling.

A small, ageing man in a dark suit was shuffling towards them in the gloom and seemed to be punching himself in the groin. The sounds he was making began to sort themselves out into: "Bitches. Dirty bitches."

Annie realised what was happening and began to laugh quietly. She turned back to look at Kirsty, who, by now, was spitting out her doughring. Annie caught Eileen's eye, who also began to laugh, but Kirsty had a wild look on her face.

"Get away. Get away," she yelled, and raised her arm, threw her doughring in his direction. It landed about six paces in front of him and bounced harmlessly against a gravestone.

Annie, shocked at the waste said, "What the Hell did you do that for?"

Eileen's head was right back, laughter gurgling in her throat. The old man, discomfited by the drama, half turned away.

"You silly bitch. I was wanting that doughring," said Annie.

At the sight of the retreating figure, and sobered by Annie's anger, Kirsty said, "Well bloody well buy your own."

Annie became aware of her cigarette and saw that distraction and the wind had virtually finished it.

"Shite," she said, and dropped it on the flattened soil. Eileen was still giggling and slapped Kirsty on the back.

Rosemary Mackay

"Wis it nae big enough for you, Kirsty. Would you rather he'd been better pleased wi' us?"

Kirsty angrily shrugged Eileen off.

"It was uninvited," she said.

Rosemary Mackay
Original Prints, Polygon (1985)

Cold Kebab Breakfast

There's a load of Indian places down Lothian Road. It's just as well. The first one we passed was closed; the second one had two big bouncers that shook their heads and flexed their biceps at us; but the third one came up trumps. As we walked in the door, a waiter came running up to us.

Table for three, I said.

No, he replied.

Table for three, *please*, said Jugger.

Sorry, said the waiter, We're full-up.

There's an empty table over there, I said

No, it's booked! The waiter looked at his watch. Party arriving in ten minutes.

Well, we'll eat quick, laughed Jugger. I'm fucking starving pal: could eat a horse!

So that's one tandoori horse, said Ivan, and a couple of nans as well. . . .

Look, said the waiter loudly, his arms out to stop Ivan and Jugger breenging past him, You can have a carry-out, but there's no tables at all. Carry-out only, Here's the menu, please take a seat.

He waved us over onto a row of plastic chairs in an alcove by the door. We sat down and started looking at the selection.

Do they do anything vegetarian? said Jugger. Cause I'm a vegetable myself, and I'm not into being a cannibal. . . . He laughed, then hiccuped, bouncing up off his seat slightly. When he landed it was right on the edge of his chair, and he started to slide off slowly away from us. Suddenly he tipped right over and thumped onto the floor.

Me and Ivan looked at him. Should we get him up? I said

No, he's safer there, said Ivan. As long as nobody trips up and spills red-hot vindaloo over him.

We looked back at the menu. After a second I found I couldn't concentrate on the reading cause I was bursting for a pish. I'm off to the bog, I said, and weaved away across the restaurant. It was fucking packed, but I only bumped into a couple of elbows on the way,.

When I came out of the lavvy, I paused for a second trying to remember where I'd been sitting. As I was looking around, I spotted somebody I kent at a table over by the window. She was beautiful, absolutely beautiful. She'd been beautiful when I'd met her before—at a party I'd crashed in Fountainbridge somewhere—but she was even more beautiful now. I don't know what it was, whether it was something she'd done to her hair and her eyes, or whatever clothes she had on, or maybe something I'd been drinking, but I felt myself drawn towards her, sucked across the restaurant, my eyes glued to her face and the forkful of chicken korma she was lifting to her mouth. At that moment my greatest wish in life was to be a lump of chicken korma.

I knelt down beside her, wobbling a bit. I put my hand on her leg to steady myself, and looked up, smiling: smiling and almost greeting as well, she was that beautiful.

Christ, Dilys, I said, It's great to see you again! My God you're looking barrie! It's a Christmas present seeing you here, that's what it is: bloody magic! I just . . . Christ, I love you Dilys, I just do, I love you.

She looked down at me. My name's Nicola, she said. I think you've got the wrong person.

Nicola, Nicola! Of course! What did I say? Dilys? Christ, what a fucking numptie, eh! It's just I was so carried away there: you're so fucking beautiful! Even more than before!

I don't think I know you at all, she said, taking a grip on her fork and hovering it over my hand on her leg. I must've been gripping her knee too hard; I leant against the edge of the table instead.

Nicola, come on! That one night! We were getting on great. Down by Marco's, mind? I loved you then even, I just couldn't say it: I was kind of shy, mind, cause you'd caught me smuggling that bottle of bleach out of the bog and I was going to put it in the punch!

Oh aye, said Nicola. I remember you now.

Sure you do!

Aye, I do. So could you just get out of my sight right away?

But I love you Nicola, I really do! I know it's short notice, but come on, let's get married: now! We'll get the head waiter to do it.

It's impossible, she said. I'm married already. This is my husband here, and my mother-in-law.

I looked at the other folk sitting at the table. I'd kind of forgotten they were there, I was that carried away. Hello! I said. Christ, you're a lucky man, married to Dilys here: fucking gorgeous! Here, if you're ever getting divorced, let me know, eh! Ha ha ha!

The husband had a funny look on his face, as if he was about to go totally fucking radge at any second for some reason. And the mother was looking a bit stunned as well: maybe she'd just bit into a chilli or something. I looked back at Dilys, no, Nicola again. She had a grain of rice stuck to her top lip right at the corner of her mouth. I reached up with my pointy finger to brush it off, a friendly kind of move, but something went wrong, she jerked herself away, and I got a jolt off her chair and my finger went out of control and poked her in the eye. She yowled.

Oh Christ, I'm sorry! I jumped up, grabbed a napkin off the table and tried to push it against her eye as a kind of pad. She shrieked again, started swinging her arms at me. Her husband stood up. I think it's time you left pal, he said. His mother was shouting, Waiter, waiter, waiter! And I was beginning to get the feeling that I'd offended somebody in some way. Eh, maybe if you put some water on the napkin it'll cool it down, I said, picking up the jug from the middle of the table. Then somebody shouted my name.

Pockie! Come on you bastard! It was Ivan across by the door. He was pointing at Jugger, who was just walking out with two carrier bags of foil boxes of grub.

I turned back to the table. I'm afraid I'll have to love you and leave you, I said.

Piss off! said Nicola, no, Dilys.

I caught up with Ivan and Jugger outside. That's a hell of a carry-out, I said to them.

Aye, I went for the set meal for six in the end, said Ivan.

But there's only three of us. . . .

Aye, but I wanted onion bhajis, you see, and you didn't get them with the three-person thing. Anyway, I'm fucking starving!

Jugger stopped. I'm fucking starved as well, he said. Come on, let's have a bit of it now, there's plenty for later.

Best to get it hot anyway, I said, and took one of the carriers off him.

We sat down on the doorstep of a shop, and spread the boxes out on the pavement in front of us. The problem is how to know which is what, said Ivan.

Only one way to find out, said Jugger. He picked up the container nearest him, started to peel the lid off, then screamed, Aiya fucker! and flung the box away from him, red sauce and steam streaming out. Fucking

117

burnt me you bastard! he shouted, and started blowing on the back of his hand, which had splashes of sauce over it.

That looked like a bhuna to me, I said.

What! Jugger, you dopey cunt, said Ivan. I was looking forward to the fucking bhuna, that's my favourite you bastard!

Well tough shit! I'm probably fucking scarred for life cause of your fucking bhuna.

I'll fucking scar you! said Ivan, jumping to his feet and kicking a couple of containers away across the pavement. I'm going to have to eat some of your creamy Persian prawn shite now: milky fucking skitters you bastard!

Look, settle, settle, I said. Let's get stuck into what we have, eh? I opened a couple of boxes. Look, here's pilau rice. Who's got the forks.

Silence.

Somebody must have them.

I thought Jugger was getting them, said Ivan, stepping from one foot to the other.

I thought Ivan was getting them, said Jugger, looking down at the rice steaming away in its boxes.

I sighed. Ach, fuck it. Look, we've still got the bhajis. Lets split them and get a taxi home. I'm shagged out with all this to be honest.

Ivan nodded slowly. Aye, I suppose so. I've got to get home and wrap up Diane's present yet. . . . He started off down the road.

I got up and headed after him. In a second, Jugger came alongside me, clutching the wee bag of onion things. Hey guys, he said, Great idea! We can get the joe baxi to stop in by the shopping centre, and we'll get a kebab to take home with us. I think there's a bottle of Grouse under our tree. Well, I fucking ken there is: I bought it for my old man. He won't mind us having a wee sup for the festive season.

I yawned. Well, I suppose it is after midnight probably. . . .

Aye, fucking magic! Merry Christmas here we come! Jugger walked out into the road and started whistling through his fingers, waving down full taxis as they skiffed by him at top speed.

Then an empty joe appeared and stopped, and we got in. It was a woman driving. Where to? she said.

All the way darling! shouted Ivan, and him and Jugger started laughing and carrying on: kissing the glass partition and stuff.

After a minute the driver looked in her mirror and said, Okay, one last chance lads: where to?

Jugger and Ivan were still laughing and mucking about, trying to get each other's trousers down or something, and they paid her no heed. So I leant forward and told her where we were going.

Before I'd finished speaking even the taxi pulled away with a lurch and I was flung backwards onto the others; they shoved me off, shouting abuse, and I was tumbled onto the floor of the cab as it zoomed round in a U-turn right across Lothian Road, and sped off northwards.

There was a faint smell of sickness down on the floor, and also something else, a kind of burnt oil smell, but on the whole it wasn't too uncomfortable. It even had a carpet. I decided I might as well just stay lying there for all the time it would take us getting home.

So I lay there, looking up at Jugger and Ivan fighting on the seat, seeing streetlamps and lit-up buses passing by the back window. There was a bit of a rhythm to the bumping of the road and the grinding of the gears, and soon it was lulling me off to sleep.

And there as I lay, half-dozing, half-waking, I saw a vision of Christmas future, a premonition of what was surely to come. Clear as day I saw me lying in my bed on Christmas morning, still in my clothes under the covers, a pint of water on the bedside unit. And as I struggle awake, rubbing open my eyes, a strange strong smell prickles my nostrils. I look round. My right hand is clutching something on the pillow, a large-sized doner, one bite out of the end, lettuce and onions and strips of greasy meat dribbling down onto the sheets: cold kebab breakfast.

Duncan McLean (b. 1964)
Bucket of Tongues, Secker & Warburg (1992)

The Lost Chip Shop

When I was a kid living in the Townhead district of Glasgow, my brother and myself used to go to a cinema on the South Side. We usually preferred The Elephant because it was the grandest on the bus route, with huge hand-tinted photographs of Alan Ladd and Ava Gardner framed in improbable gilt plasterwork on the foyer walls. And when an usherette eventually discovered us halfway through the second sitting of the B Western and pitched us out into the street, it was always an incredible shock to find that it was dark outside, the street lights illuminating a steady drizzle, and giving a homely, city effect in the bright reflections of the shopfronts.

It'd be about 5.30 and we would already be late and in for trouble when we got home but it was nice coming out of the flicks into the evening rain, with people hurrying homewards, their breath propelling out of their nostrils like St George's dragon in the book illustrations, and wee women doing the shopping on the way, stuffing cauliflowers into bucket bags.

My brother and I would walk down to a particular chip shop and buy a fourpenny bag of chips which we'd share while we waited for the 104 bus to take us back to Townhead. We always went to this chip shop as their chips were the best we knew—dry and golden, crisp on the outside and powdery on the inside.

But what I really liked about the shop was the inside of it. It had rows of wooden cubicles, rather like the bars you saw in gangster films. That was where you sat if you bought a fish tea. A fish tea consisted of a large plate of fish and chips, a mug of wonderfully stewed tea, and several slices of margarined co-op Gold Medal bread. You 'sat in' for this; a quaint phrase, as though you were Charlie Parker at a gig.

There were people who ate there every night, because the food was cheap, plentiful and good. In the Depression, I'm told, the chip shop provided an inexpensive, tasty meal, and even a bit of a night out. It might puff you up unnaturally, and make you old and fat before your time, but it kept you alive.

This shop had been there a long time, and it had always been run by Enrico and his wife, a stout little woman with thick grey hair, and

Mediterranean eyes as brilliant as drops of black coffee. Despite the fact that they had been in Britain for perhaps 20 or so years, they spoke English only haltingly, but they were always courteous and friendly, and everybody liked them.

It wasn't though, just the people who ran the shop which made this our usual port of call, nor the wonderful smell of cooking oil and vinegar. It was the big fish-frying machine itself. It lay against the wall opposite the counter like a great Wurlitzer organ, like an enormous ark of convenant in a wealthy synagogue. Made of chrome and opalescent glass, it was polished until it gleamed.

Both Enrico and his wife were very small and so they had made a wooden step on which they stood as they shifted the chips around in the vats of oil. That even added to the ritualistic, almost sacramental, appearance of the great machine. They looked like two high priests at an altar, swinging the monstrance. And the question which they always asked, as they piled your chips into the newspaper, sounded vaguely religious as well, "saul anna vinegar?" they would inquire, in the same tone of voice as a priest saying mass might use.

But in the middle of this great ark, right across the length of it, was a huge panorama of a painting, protected by a curving sheet of Perspex. It was a picture of some beauty spot in Enrico's native Naples. The painting was rather inexpertly done, but it had a freshness for all that—rather like the work of Raoul Duffy.

The scene looked out across the Bay of Naples from the vantage point of a quiet, white-washed loggia. There were cypress and olive trees. The sky was a light blue and, from the way that the red roofs reflected the sun, I always imagined that it was about ten o' clock in the morning. And I have never been able to get that picture out of my head.

For when I eat spaghetti, I know the loggia lies freshly white-washed just outside the kitchen door. Whenever I eat in the more expensive Italian restaurants, everything looks so fake with all those Chianti bottles and plastic vines, in comparison to Enrico's chip shop. For all their pretensions, the exhorbitant trattorias don't feel like Italy, and Enrico's did.

I say it did, for it is all changed now. The last time I looked for the place I couldn't find it at first. Eventually, in place of the old marbled exterior, I found a modern Fish 'n' Chicken bar.

A sinking feeling grew in my stomach as I entered the Alcan doors.

The place was retina-shattering bright. Working-class places usually are, as though the colour control knob has been turned up high. Everything was bright; the Formica, the glossy ceiling, the two young owners—and the fish frying machine. It sparkled at every point of its glass and steel frontage, at every lip of its Germanic, characterless, hulk. There was no vaguely Art-Deco opalescent glass with a square picture house clock set in it. And there was no picture of Naples Bay. A wave of despair swept over me. This was no triumphant ark, only a stainless steel coffin, with a darkness all around it, despite the glare.

The ark had gone, and so had Enrico and his stout little wife with the eyes like black coffee. They had gone back to Italy, to Naples, no doubt to sit in a quiet white-washed loggia high above the bay. God knows how often Enrico thought of that place as looked at the picture and shifted the chips around. It must be difficult for him now, in a way, over in Italy, for he spent more than thirty years in a grey northern industrial city where it rained and grew dark as you came out of the pictures. And perhaps, you never know, he now sits out, in his place in the sun, and occasionally looks at a picture of a dark street somewhere in Glasgow with the street lights reflecting in the rain.

Jack McLean
The Bedside Urban Voltaire
Lochar (1990)

'Tibby was for cutting it in twa cuts, but I like a saumon to be served up in its integrity.'

Christopher North
Noctes Ambrosianae (1822-1835)

Adam McNaughtan

The Jeely Piece Song

I'm a skyscraper wean; I live on the nineteenth flair,
But I'm no' gaun oot tae play ony mair,
'Cause since we moved tae Castlemilk, I'm wastin' away
'Cause I'm gettin' wan meal less every day:

Chorus
> *Oh ye cannae fling pieces oot a twenty storey flat*
> *Seven hundred hungry weans'll testify to that.*
> *If it's butter, cheese or jeely,*
> > *if the breid is plain or pan,*
> *The odds against it reaching earth*
> > *are ninety-nine to wan.*

On the first day ma maw flung oot a daud o' Hovis
                        broon;
It came skytin' oot the windae and went up
                        insteid of o' doon.
Noo every twenty-seven hoors it comes back intae sight
'Cause ma piece went intae orbit and became a satellite.

On the second day ma maw flung me
                        a piece oot wance again.
It went and hut the pilot in a fast low-flying plane.
He scraped it aff his goggles,
                        shouting through the intercom,
'The Clydeside Reds huv goat me
                        wi' a breid-and-jeely bomb.'

On the third day ma maw thought
                she would try another throw.
The Salvation Army band was staunin' doon below.
'Onward, Christian Soldiers' was the piece
                they should've played
But the oompah man was playing a piece an'
                marmalade.

We've wrote to Oxfam to try an' get some aid,
An' a the weans in Castlemilk
                have formed a 'piece brigade.'
We're gonnae march to George's Square
                demanding civil rights
Like nae mair hooses ower piece-flinging height.

Adam McNaughtan (1967)
in *Mungo's Tongues,* Mainstream (1994)

She put into the carriage a basket of excellent gooseberries, and
some of the finest apricots I ever saw or tasted, which have grown
out of doors; the season has been unusually favourable and her
husband was fond of cultivating his garden.

Robert Southey at Inverness
Journal of a Tour in Scotland in 1819

Nettle Kail

This simple but delicious soup is associated specially with the month of March, when nettles are young and fresh and the black March cockerel is exactly a year old, with young and tender flesh. The nettles were picked commonly on the old drystones dykes or the walls of the drystone-built 'black' houses, now rapidly vanishing. In the old days, March time was tonic time, and it was believed that nettle kail, taken three times a during the month—sometimes on three consecutive days—purified the blood, learned the complexion, and in general, ensured good health during the ensuing year. Shrove Tuesday was a very special night for a nettle kail supper. All the members of the family were expected to be present, and a blessing was invoked on the spring work.

Rachel Macleod, Barra,
(in a letter to the author, accompanying the recipe)

A year-old cockerel, young nettles, oat or barley meal, butter, salt, pepper, wild garlic or onion or mint, water.

Gather a sufficient quantity of young nettles from the higher part of the wall, where they are clean. (It is advisable to wear gloves). Strip off the young, tender leaves at the top (discarding coarser ones), and wash in several changes of salted water. Dry in a clean cloth and chop finely, unless the leaves are very small. Put the dressed and stuffed bird into the kail-pot the two quarts of cold water. Bring slowly to the boil, and add the nettles—about three-quarters of a pint—and a handful of oat or barley meal, stirring well. Add salt to taste, a good pat of butter, and a little wild garlic, onion or mint, as preferred. Simmer until the bird is tender then season the kail to taste.

For the stuffing, rub a piece of butter into twice its weight in oatmeal or barley meal, or substitute finely chopped suet for the butter. Season with salt, pepper and a little wild garlic or mint (fresh or powdered). Mix the ingredients well and stuff the bird. Insert a skewer in the opening.

In some districts whole barley is substituted for meal, but it should then be put on in cold water. Nettles make an excellent substitute for spinach in early spring.

F Marian McNeill
The Scots Kitchen, its lore and recipes, Blackie (1929)

Living off Nature

We had an appetite for dinner. Game formed the staple of this meal. Sometimes Terry pot-roasted a bit of venison haunch and made a sort of Yorkshire pudding to accompany the meat; generally she stewed the venison; we had venison and grouse, blue hill hares and an occasional rabbit, black-cock, snipe, duck, plover and roe-deer. We had not lack of quantity and variety so far as meat was concerned. As soon as the blaeberries ripened we added them to our dinner. Terry often made soup of a bone; we hunted the country round for green stuff to put in the broth.

Our garden of nettles which grew over the ruins of an old house was quickly stripped. We cooked the nettles like cabbage and used the water in which they were boiled amongst our soups. The nettle-pottage tasted as sweet as cabbage, but it came to an end. We tried many queer messes thereafter, young grass in the soup, birch leaves cooked like cabbage. We attempted to eat the latter dish once only. But when we flung away the mess of boiled birch leaves I recalled a trick of my boyhood. I made slots in the bark of some birch trees and collected the spilling sap that flowed from these cuts in milk-tins nailed to the trunks of trees. We supped the sap with a teaspoon as if it was medicine, and felt that it was doing us good.

"Spring's the time for the sap," I told Terry.

"We'll need it then," she said.

We dug up the small nuts that grow at the root of a white-flowered plant on grassy slopes, as I used to when I was a boy.

The arrival of ripe blaeberries saved us from worrying about scurvy.

"And after them come crowberries." I said, "and cranberries then, and cloudberries. Terry, before we lack we'll go down to the fields at Kinlochlaggan or Laggan Bridge and steal turnips, like our neighbours the deer."

"We'll have to," she said simply.

When we had eaten dinner we bathed in Loch Coulter. If there was time to spare before bright day arrived we set a line for pike. We took food once again in mid-morning. We gave ourselves a precious bannock of oatcake spread thinly with jam or thickly with deer-fat, or we had scones that Terry baked on the griddle. We drank water.

We often say, in wonder-struck tones after a plain bare meal, that we never felt so well in all our lives before.

Ian MacPherson (1905-44)
Wild Harbour, Methuen (1936)

. . . Dined sumptuously upon venison, a piece of Roe, dressed partly in Collops with sauce, and partly on the grid-iron.

Robert Forbes
Diaries 1708-1775

Barrack Brose

In these barracks the food is of the plainest and coarsest description: oatmeal forms its staple, with milk, when milk can be had, which is not always: and as the men have to cook by turns, with only half an hour or so given them in which to light a fire, and prepare the meal for a dozen or twenty associates, the cooking is invariably an exceedingly rough and simple affair. I have known mason-parties engaged in the central Highlands in building bridges, not unfrequently reduced by a tract of wet weather, that soaked their only fuel the turf and rendered it incombustible, to the extremity of eating their oatmeal raw, and merely moistened by a little water, scooped by the hand from a neighbouring brook.

Hugh Miller (1802-56)
My Schools and Schoolmasters (1854)

The Kindly House

Kirstie beckoned to Catherine: "Come, you and I will get a supper tray, my soul. I must see are the larders so well stocked as they were when we weans would go thieving."

Margaret Bearcrofts said: "Aye, I am as hungry as a March ewe. See you bring enough for us all, Aunt Kirstie, for I doubt we mostly had poor appetites earlier on." And then she called after them: "You are forgetting the larder will be locked!"

At that all three laughed, but there was a shaken edge to it that was near tears.

"Mrs Grizzie is aye hiding the key in a different place," said Margaret, "but I think you will discover it if you dip your hand into the barley in the blue crock."

On their way through each took one of the heavy oaken trays from Tammie's pantry. In the blink of the two candles it was all neat and damp; the copper-bound wooden tubs for the washing of glasses were standing bottom up. They left a candle there to light them along the stone passage and lighted others in the kitchen sconces. They both of them felt the need of lights and both of them wondered under what hedge poor Mr Strange might be sheltering.

There was still a glow of red in the ashes and Catherine threw on some light wood and coals and worked with the bellows till it flared up. Easy enough to heat up the tail of the soup with a measure or so of milk in it and the cooked peas for thickening. Aye, there was the key sure enough and Kirstie went down to the larder on tiptoe, playing robbers and reivers as she used to as a wean with wee Rob, and with Jamie and Ann who were so long dead that now it was no pain to think on them, but rather joy of old happiness remembered. The candle flickered in a cold draught, but she found the pie and a piece of ham, fresh cheese, butter in a cloth and a batch of scones, as much as she could carry, almost. Beyond, in the corner of the larder, was tomorrow's gigot and a bundle of teals, ready to be plucked and trussed in the forenoon. When they were weans it was always the sweet stuff they were after, raisins best of all when there were any. She could not mind on so muckle fresh meat; when they killed a sheep or a young stot, it would be a day to talk

129

on. Everything needed to go farther and not near the same imported stuff to fall back on.

In the kitchen, Catherine had the broth hotting up over the fire. She had taken a handful of almonds out of a jar and was sitting on the table, nibbling away at them. It was a good high kitchen with plenty head room for the hams and flitches and onions and the bunches of fresh dipped candles hanging butt down.

"When I was a bairn," said Kirstie, "there was never the same kind of profusion as here. We werena just so secure over food. If there was a bad har'st we might all begin to fare badly, and worse if it was two years running. Now you will get folks scarcely knowing or caring how the har'st has gone."

Naomi Mitchison (b. 1897)
The Bull Calves, Cape (1947)

Noami Mitchison's novel *The Bull Calves* is set in Perthshire after the Forty-five and based on her own family history.

Crowdie

Set pan with freshly sour or thick milk on a slow heat and watch till it curdles, not letting it simmer or boil or it will harden. When set, let it cook before drawing off the whey. Use a muslin cloth. When whey is completely squeezed out mix crowdie with a little salt until you find it very soft in your hands, mix with cream or top of milk and set out in dishes. The mixture can also be pressed in a colander to remove whey and a weight placed on top. The crowdie can then be sliced like cheese.

Anonymous, undated, manuscript recipes from Lewis

Hunger

in that room there is a mirror
and in that mirror there is a room
and in that room there is a land of candles
and in that land there is a lake of coffee
and in that lake there is an island of ananas au kirsch
and in that island there is a spring of prunelle de bourgogne
and in that spring there is a log of hanche de chevreuil
and in that log there is a sap of givry clos st pierre
and in that sap there is a node of petite fondue
and in that node there is a drop of juliénas
and in that drop there is a cell of pochouse seurroise
and in that cell there is a gel of rully blanc
and in that gel there is a nucleus of galantine de jambon
and in that nucleus there is a stain of mâcon lugny
and in that stain there is a map of skin
and in that map there is a land of rags
and in that land there is a room of bones
and in that room there is a mirror
in that mirror there is a room

Edwin Morgan (b. 1920)
Collected Poems, Carcanet (1990)

Strawberries

There were never strawberries
like the ones we had
that sultry afternoon
sitting on the step
of the open french window
facing each other
your knees held in mine
the blue plates in our laps
the strawberries glistening
in the hot sunlight
we dipped them in sugar
looking at each other
not hurrying the feast
for one to come
the empty plates
laid on the stone together
with the two forks crossed
and I bent towards you
sweet in that air
in my arms
abandoned like a child
from your eager mouth
the taste of strawberries
in my memory
lean back again
let me love you

let the sun beat
on our forgetfulness
one hour of all
the heat intense
and summer lightning
on the Kilpatrick hills

let the storm wash the plates

Edwin Morgan (b. 1920)
Collected Poems, Carcanet (1990)

Flight

One day off-handedly her sister told her
she was fat. Sixteen years old,
construing her adolescence in the mirror
and deciding she objected to the mould
and curve of breast and thigh,
she took to muesli, oranges and lettuce,
lost thirty pounds in sixty days
tucking in jeans instead of food. 'Don't fuss,'
she told her mother, who called it 'Just a phase'.
Father, table-thumping, predicted she would die.

Thin as a sparrow, secretive as a water-rail,
with pointed nose and elongated toes,
she pecked her food, grew pale,
sprouted fingered wings and rose
one day from family noise and bother
to flutter through the open kitchen window,
circling and soaring high into the sky.
Father preoccupied failed to see her go.
Mother remarked, 'I'm not surprised. Our Di
ate just like a bird.' 'How absurd!' said Father.

Mother it was who missed her most, pattering
round the house beslippered every evening,
leaving the cage-door open and scattering
bird-seed on a plate. But too little and too late.

Ken Morrice
When Truth is Known, AUP (1986)

David Morrison

Wyster Gut Cure

Dear Scott,

What a weekend I've had with this totally obnoxious English poet who suddenly turned up on our doorstep saying that he had been told I would put him up because I was a kindred sprit and I had been recommended by you know who; yes James Scaddon, that little prick who has used and abused my hospitality again and again, and then he had the audacity to give a bad review to the last book. The wee fart! I went along with this person and believe it or not I think I could quite possibly market our fare for English poetical aching gut. This 5' 6" arrogant little puerile poet (his work is really self indulgent shit) actually 'phoned from Glasgow thanking me and Fiona for our care and attention saying that his gut was now well and truly sorted out, vowing never to go back to chips, fastfood crap, Chinese or Indian takeaways etc.

There was no mention of course about repayment of the £20 I gave him to help him get back to London. Why am I taken in again and again by these folk? It would have been tolerably o.k. if he was able to write. Ochone! Ochone!

Well, Scott, I shall briefly relate the weekend to you.

Our fare here in the north I believe is the best in the world. Simple and good.

He arrived at 8.30 p.m. on Friday. His hair was greasy. His clothes were greasy and he was clutching a brown paper bag which contained half-eaten greasy chips. Showed him his room. He had a shower and then came down for a chat. Gave him a whisky. He usually drinks beer but I suggested while here he should drink the real stuff. For supper we had a bowl of MOOSHIE PEAS, TOAST and TEA then another whisky. I suggested an early night, but he went out for a walk. As his guts had been acting up recently. In the morning I gave him a cup of hot water followed by WHOLEGRAIN TOAST and MARMALADE with a CUP OF TEA, followed by PORRIDGE AND BRAN with MILK. After that he was hardly able to move. He commented on the water. Ay, we have the best of water here. Remember the Portuguese who came to stay for a day or so. They raved about the water and filled numerous bottles for their journey west.

As I was writing a new short story which had a deadline, I worked for a few hours and we had a late lunch which consisted of HERRING done in oatmeal, a little side salad. He felt like a rest in the afternoon so I got on with the writing. Before dinner we had a whisky then HOMEMADE CARROT SOUP, followed by COLD SALMON and little JOHN O' GROAT TATTIES. I'm afraid that being with him and trying to converse intelligently was quite an endurance test as his knowledge of Scottish history and literature was so minimal that it hardly existed. Fiona was polite as is her norm but stayed out of the way as much as possible. For supper she made some FLOUER SCONES, (the ground flour from the local mill). We had a couple with a cup of tea. By now the poet was in ecstasies about our fare. His eating habits centre around junk food. Before he went to bed, with a sigh of contentment he stated that his guts were far more settled now. He would really get a good night's sleep.

On Sunday he refused the porridge and bran and just had the tea and toast. He really enjoyed the bread which is from the local bakers and the not the supermarket. Then something which nearly gave me gut pains . . . I had to endure an hour or so of his reading his own poetry. Did I say poetry?

Naturally I called his work INTERESTING. As you know I never review work. I prefer not to offend.

Again we had a late lunch which consisted of a SIMPLE OMELETTE, SALAD BREAD AND BUTTER. The eggs were naturally free range, local ones. In the afternoon I had to write so he went walking, returning in time for dinner. He expounded on the delights of the area, the cliffs, the birdlife. He had already started writing some poems. Oh, God, no, thought I. For dinner, his last meal with us, thank God, was PRIME LOCAL VENISON, REDCURRANT SAUCE, LOCAL BROCCOLI with JOHN O' GROAT TATTIES. He said that he had never eaten so well before and his guts were truly marvellous! Naturally, with his type, he never even gave Fiona a box of chocolates or me a bottle or half bottle of whisky. A right user of the worst kind. I suggested that he should get the early morning bus and this he did clutching two bottles of water, salad sandwiches and my £20.00 His thanks was so profuse that it was sickening. He categorically stated that he would eat properly in the future but it was difficult with him doing so much travelling, meeting different people. Most of them seemed to eat junk food. When I suggested that he should just stay at home and eat properly, Fiona found it really hard to contain a loud burst of laughter. He was too thick to see what I really meant.

But then, wait for it! I almost shat myself. Finally he said, "I'll have to tell all my friends, especially if they have got an aching gut to come and see you". I and Fiona said nothing. God, what a life!

Yours Aye
    Dad

David Morrison (b. 1941)
(previously unpublished)

P.E.N. Punch

Rub the rinds of five lemons with lump sugar, using half a pound of sugar. Put the lemony sugar in a bowl, add a bottle of old rum, then the strained juice of the lemons, and mix well. Put in a piece of cinnamon stick, and pour on the boiling water, stirring all the time.

Mr W.G. Burn-Murdoch's recipe
from *The Scots Week-end*
edited by Donald and Catherine Carswell (Routledge, 1936)

A Vegetarian Experiment

The *Vital Spark* had been lying for some time in the Clyde getting a new boiler, and her crew, who had been dispersed about the city in their respective homes, returned to the wharf on a Monday morning to make ready for a trip to Tobermory.

"She's a better boat than ever she was," said Macphail with satisfaction, having made a casual survey. "Built like a lever watch! We'll can get the speed oot o' her noo. There's boats gaun up and doon the river wi' red funnels, saloon cabins, and German bands in them, that havena finer engines. When I get that crank and crossheid tightened, thae glands packed and nuts slacked, she'll be the gem o' the sea."

"She's chust sublime!" said Para Handy, patting the tarred old hull as if he were caressing a kitten; "it's no' coals and timber she should be carryin' at aal, but towrist passengers. Man! if we chust had the accommodation!"

"Ye should hae seen the engines we had on the *Cluthas!*" remarked Sunny Jim, who had no illusions about the *Vital Spark* in that respect. "They were that shiney I could see my face in them."

"Could ye, 'faith?" said Macphail; "a sicht like that must have put ye aff yer work. We're no' that fond o' polish in the coastin' tred that we mak' oor engines shine like an Eyetalian ice-cream shop; it's only vanity. Wi' us it's speed—"

"Eight knots," murmured Sunny Jim, who was in a nasty Monday-morning humour. "Eight knots, and the chance o' nine wi' wind and tide."

"You're a liar!" said the Captain irritably, "and that's my advice to you. Ten knots many a time between the Cloch and the Holy Isle," and an argument ensued which it took Dougie all his tact to put an end to short of bloodshed.

"It's me that's gled to be back on board of her anyway," remarked Para Handy later; "suppose you'll soon be gettin' the dinner ready, Jum? See and have something nice, for I'm tired o' sago puddin'."

"Capital stuff for pastin' up bills," said Dougie; "I've seen it often in the cookin'-depots. Was the wife plyin' ye wi' sago?"

"Sago, and apples, potatoes, cabbage, cheese, and a new kind o'

137

patent coffee that agrees wi' the indigestion; I havena put my two eyes on a bit of Christian beef since I went ashore; the wife's in wan of her tirravees, and she's turned to be a vegetarian."

"My Chove!" said Dougie incredulously; "are you sure, Peter?"

"Sure enough! I told her this morning when I left I would bring her home a bale of hay from Mull, and it would keep her goin' for a month or two. Women's a curious article!"

"You should get the munister to speak to her," said Dougie sympathetically. "When a wife goes wrong like that, there's nothing bates the munister. She'll no' be goin' to the church; it's aalways in the way wi' them fancy new releegions. Put you her at wance in the hands o' a dacent munister."

"I canna be harsh wi' her, or she'll greet," said Para Handy sadly.

"It's no harshness that's wanted," counselled the mate, speaking from years of personal experience; "what you need iss to be firm. What way did this calamity come on her? Don't be standin' there, Jum, like a soda-water bottle, but hurry and make a bit of steak for the Captain; man! I noticed you werena in trum whenever I saw you come on board. I saw at wance you hadn't the agility. What way did the trouble come on her?"

"She took it off a neighbour woman," explained the Captain. "She was aal right on the Sunday, and on the Monday mornin' she couldna bear to look at ham and eggs. It might happen to anybody. The thing was at its heid when I got home, and the only thing on the table wass a plate of maccaroni."

"Eyetalian!" chimed in the engineer. "I've seen them makin' it in Genoa and hingin' it up to bleach on the washin' greens. It's no' meat for men; it's only for passin' the time o' organ-grinders and ship-riggers."

"'Mery,' I said to her, 'I never saw nicer decorations, but hurry up like a darlin' wi' the meat.' 'There'll be no more meat in this hoose, Peter,' she said, all trumblin; 'if you saw them busy in a slaughter-hoose you wadna eat a chop. Forbye, there's uric acid in butcher meat, and there's more nourishment in half a pound o' beans than there iss in half a bullock.' 'That's three beans for a sailor's dinner; it's no' for nourishment a man eats always; half the time it's only for amusement, Mery,' said I to her, but it wass not the time for argyment. 'You'll be a better man in every way if you're a vegetarian,' she said to me. 'If it iss a better man you are wantin', I says to her, wonderful caalm in my temper, 'you are on the right tack, sure enough; you have only to go on with them expuriments wi' my meat and you'll soon be a weedow woman.'

"But she wouldna listen to reason, Mery, and for a fortnight back I have been feedin' like the Scribes and Sadducees in the Scruptures."

"Man! iss it no chust desperate?" said Dougie compassionately, and he admiringly watched his Captain a little later make the first hearty meal for a fortnight. "You're lookin' a dufferent man already," he told him; "what's for tea, Jum?"

"I kent a vegetarian yince," said Sunny Jim, "and he lived maist o' the time on chuckie soup."

"Chucken soup?" repeated Dougie interrogatively.

"No; chuckie soup. There was nae meat o' any kind in't. A' ye needed was some vegetables, a pot o' hot water, and a parteecular kind o' chuckie-stane. It was fine and strengthenin'."

"You would need good teeth for't, I'm thinkin'," remarked the Captain dubiously.

"Of course ye didna eat the chuckie-stane," Sunny Jum explained: "it made the stock; it was instead o' a bane, and it did ower and ower again."

"It would be a great savin'," said Dougie, fascinated with the idea. "Where do you get them parteecular kinds of chuckies?"

"Onywhere under high water," replied Sunny Jim, who saw prospects of a little innocent entertainment.

"We'll get them the first time we're ashore, then," said the mate, "and if they're ass good ass what you say, the Captain could take home a lot of them for his vegetarian mustress."

At the first opportunity, when he got ashore, Sunny Jim perambulated the beach and selected a couple of substantial pieces of quartz, and elsewhere bought a pound of margarine which he put in his pocket. "Here yez are, chaps—the very chuckie! I'll soon show ye soup," he said, coming aboard with the stones, in which the crew showed no little interest. .

"A' ye have to do is to scrub them weel, and put them in wi' the vegetables when the pot's boilin'."

They watched his culinary preparations closely. He prepared the water and vegetables, cleaned the stones, and solemnly popped them in the pot when the water boiled. At a moment when their eyes were off him he dexterously added the unsuspected pound of margarine.

By and by the soup was ready, and when dished, had all the aspects of the ordinary article. Sunny Jim himself was the first to taste it *pour encourager les autres.*

"Fair champion!" he exclaimed.

The engineer could not be prevailed to try the soup on any consideration, but the Captain and the mate had a plate apiece, and voted it extraordinary.

"It's a genius you are, Jum!" said the delighted Captain; "if the folk in Gleska knew that soup like this was to be made from chuckie-stanes they wouldna waste their time at the Fair wi' gaitherin' cockles."

And the next time Para Handy reached the Clyde he had on board in all good faith a basket-load of stones culled from the beach at Tobermory for his vegetarian mistress.

Neil Munro (1864-1930)
In Highland Harbours with Para Handy, Blackwood (1911)

Stag's Head Soup

Take two head, also the necks: soak the heads in water for one night; keep them on in a stock pot with water. When the scum rises to the top skim it all off nicely; then put in carrots, turnips and onions, celery, thyme, and bay leaves (three). Boil all the goodness out of the heads; take a piece of the cheek and press it; strain off the soup and put it away to get cold; then take off the fat, clarify the soup, and reduce it to the quantity you require. Cut up the pressed cheek in nice small pieces, and place them in the tureen with some cut-up French beans just before you take the soup. Pour a glass of port wine in it; let it boil up, put in the consommé in the tureen, and serve.

Scottish Council of the British Deer Society
Venison Recipes, complied by
Mr A M McArthur of the Highland Branch

Thom Nairn

A Poem about Apples

She always liked
Having apples around.

Brown-Green-Yellow-Gold apples.
Chopped and browning in delicate dishes.
In big-light-bowls.
In sinister plastic bags
In shapeless heaps on tables.
In big brown baskets
Wide as sharp-gummed mouths
Hungry in sunny shelved corners.

She always liked apples
Around all of her rooms.

I was always grateful
They were (rarely) on the floor.
I looked for them always.
Under tables, behind armchairs:
(Drawn curtains
Moving in the draft
Still make me nervous).

The toilet, particularly,
Was always a challenge.
I'd sit edgily
Looking over my shoulder.
Under my legs.
Always expecting them.
Innocent. Smiling.
Gleaming aimlessly.

I was always cautious.
At breakfast.
At supper.
(In the dark hours before dawn.
Especially).

In the dark I'd whistle-in the dawn,
Wrapped in blankets.
Nonchalantly clutching my baseball bat.
My hearing has improved.
My sense of smell is acute.

But time passes and soon
All around me apples would be dying.
They knew I knew.
It was only a matter of time.

They skulked, crinkling as faces
And becoming colourless.
Smelling too, unavoidably, pervasively.
Of apples dying:
You could hear them
Turning to pulp and conspiring in whispers.

Dark flies would land in passing,
Stretch, relax, hold conversations,
Drink deep of dying apples.
Take off backwards
And mess up the ceiling.

Me, I still wear heavy boots in bed.
A linen mask and nose-clip.
Ear muffs, y-fronts and goggles.

I still dream badly,
Of ripe green shoots
Growing from my ears,
My nose, my groin:
Of limbs, clumsily removed in the dark,
Crinkling apples rotting
Where once were shiny eyes.

Clustered as bats
They leech to my shoulders
Hungry and black as hawks, or owls
Waiting for dawn
And minds to pick clean.

She always liked
Having apples around.
Apples around all of her rooms.

Thom Nairn (1995)
(previously unpublished)

James Nicol

To Donald MacKelvie

(On the occasion of the complimentary dinner in his honour in the
Douglas Hotel, Brodick, 20th November, 1925. Between 1908 and 1947
Donald McKelvie introduced many new varieties of potato, their names
prefixed by 'Arran'.)

> DONALD o' tattie fame —
> > "Health to MacKelvie!"
> Long shall we praise his name
> > Whilst Arranmen delve ye.
> "Arran Chief," "Arran Rose,"
> > "Comrade" and "Ally,"
> Yea, where the "Consul" grows —
> > "Health to MacKelvie!"
>
> O Arranman, beyond compare,
> Thy pride let humble poet share,
> Whilst thou sat'st in thine honoured chair,
> > The guest of many,
> I peeled your spuds, and socht for mair
> > In ilka cranny.
>
> The table groaned beneath their load
> When I sat doon, wi' thanks to God,
> That honest fare was still abroad
> > In Arran's Isle —
> Tatties and herrin', dished a la mode,
> > By cook can bile.
>
> Bethankit! I was quite in tune,
> Wi' hungry crave, ne'er staw'd by spoon!
> I had been fastin' lang ere noon,
> > And busy at it,
> 'Mang fykey jobs that wear ane door,
> > They're sae contractit.

144

Thine "Arran Chiefs" wi' burstin' skins
Cried: "Lord, man, here forget your sins!
Dig in us wi' your molar pins,
    Ye'll find us hearty,
Likewise yer freens that flaunt the fins,
    Baith salt and tarty.

"MacKelvie reared us on his ferm
To feed a man, nor do him herm,
Although at times he'd rax his arm
    Liftin' and fillin'!
Oor flesh was built to staun the term
    O' stomachs willin'.

"Maybe at times when sterved by those,
Wha ne'er can learn hoo a tattie grows,
We're shown a wart upo' oor nose,
    It's nae discredit.
Gie us the dung—even Shisken knows
    We've strength to redd it.

"There's nae boss he'rts whaur Donal' scans
The seedlin's suited for his plans!
We're raised to fill the hoosewife's pans,
    And no' jist a name!
Come, sit ye doon, ne'er fash yer han's,
    And fill up yer wame."

And then the herrin' wi' curlin' tails,
Gat up and spak' o' favourin' gales,
Whaur hunger's sel' judeecious wales
    A course, thumb-nickit,
And sooks the banes frae aff its nails
    Wi' tongues that lick it.

They bragged o' worl'-wide salty seas,
And faur-famed glorious liberties,
The million lives a spawin' frees

Frae a'e wee bit womb
To scatter roon' the Hebridees,
There to sink or soom.

The Clyde is famed for mony a fish,
Provides to fastin' man a dish —
Whitin's or flounders to yer wish,
Frae bottoms clautit,
But gi'e me herrin' clean frae the mesh,
Especially sautit.

I wadna like to cast a sneer
On ithers dinin' somewhat queer,
The bluidy banes o' kinsfolk near —
The soo, the ox.
The flesh for me's the flesh that's clear,
And free frae pox.

Ah! could ye've watch'd my joy that nicht,
To see such beauties in my sicht —
The shape, the size, the e'en fixed ticht
Wi' pickled glitter,
Describin' scenes whaur in God's sicht
Herrin' had their flitter.

Canst wonder whaur the two combine,
Your tatties and the real "Lochfyne,"
That hungry chaps sit doon to dine,
Forgettin' the worl'?
I drew my chair fornenst the byne
And made things birl.

The peelin' bing before me grew,
The herrin' skeletons, a few,
Ere I leant back and thocht o' you
Amang the crofters,
Receivin' there the honours due
To benefactors.

146

And though apairt a mile, a' maist,
Frae whaur ye sat, by respect kiss't,
I saw yer face amidst the mist,
    Same's Greiffenhagen,
Lighted with thought that proves at least
    Man's not forsaken.

And there and then I heaved a sigh,
Replete with thanks shall never die.
"Lord bless my soul! even here am I
    Receivin' favours.
Tatties like those must rank sky-high
    'Mang mankind's savours.

And Donald, man, although fell dour,
To sip at stuff that wants the po'er,
I filled a gless ootside the door —
    They ca' it water,
And drunk yer health wi' that weak scoor
    For want o' better.

And whilst nae doot in yon gran' ha',
Whaur healths frae men o' worth did fa',
The ane that pleases best o' a'
    Comes frae man's belly!
Watter or wine, all toasters saw
    A noble fella.

Donald o' tattie fame —
    "Health to MacKelvie!"
Long shall we praise his name
    Whilst Arranmen delve ye.
"Arran Chief," "Arran Rose,"
    "Comrade" and "Ally,"
Yea, where the "Consul" grows—
    "Health to MacKelvie!"

James Nicol
A Book of Arran Verse, Ardrossan: Arthur Guthrie (1930)

Penang

Barrelling along
in the blustery drizzle of December
with Richard (for once)
that quarter pace behind
I'm in love again with Glasgow
and my squat square mile
of the wild West End.

I'm by Picasso
massy and round

but Giacometti made Richard
who
might
blow
away

Such fancies are fine
in the run up to Christmas
with the 'Mata Hari'
just a brisk step away
due East on West
           Princes
in the car alarmed night

Alluring as always
the satay is tender
our noodles and fish
exquisitely spiced
coconut and ginger
an espionage of coriander
winey secrets, code word
'Medoc' which may not be
Malaysian but is warming and cheap

and goes well with chopsticks
and the torrid palette
of Hock au Teh
whose sun struck abstracts
giggle on the walls.
In season
oriental song birds
          chit chat
on the terrace but tonight
winter holds a finger to its lips
and we dine en deux, alone

Our waitress
is taking her finals
at Glasgow
In electrical engineering
but plans to go back

In the meantime she slips us clues
in the Tourist Board 'promotion'
There are fabulous prizes. . . .
so Mata Hari means 'rising sun'
Richard and I sip claret
licking garlic off our sealed lips
planning our exploits
on the lam in Penang

Donny O'Rourke (1996)
(previously unpublished)

Fed Up

See ma mammy,
says eat yer dinner.
Gies me cabbidge.
See ma granny,
says the wean
wullnae eat that,
leave it, hen.
Gies me choclit.
See ma daddy,
says ah've goatie
clear ma plate.
Dinnae like that
greasy gravy,
stane cauld tatties.
See ma granda,
says the bairn
s'no goat a stummick
like a coo.
Gies me lickris,
pandroaps, chews.
Ett thum aw.

Feel seek noo.

Janet Paisley
(previously unpublished)

This is Tomorrow

—Corn Flakes, Weetabix or Honey Smacks? the mother asked, as her daughter trotted behind her into the kitchen.

—I want porridge.

—Please.

—Porridge, *please*.

—I don't think there is any.

—Yes there is. It's in the cupboard.

—I don't think so.

—Yes it is. So there! I want porridge I want PORRIDGE! It was going to be porridge or a tantrum and porridge took less time so she put on a pan of milk to heat and began clearing away the clutter from the night before. As the milk frothed over the lip of the pan, she could hear the baby begin to cry, its whimpers building up to a full-throttled scream. She lifted the pan off the heat, stirred in the oats, turned down the gas, filled a beaker of juice for her daughter and gave her a book to look at while the porridge cooked, while she got the baby up, washed and dried its hot pink bottom, changed its nappy and dressed her in fresh clothes, threw the nightsuit into the laundry basket, slid the jiggling body into the highchair, while she filled a kettle and switched it on, found the baby's plate and beaker, cut a slice of bread for herself and put it under the grill to toast. She dropped a dollop of porridge in the Peter Rabbit bowl, added milk, sugar, spoon, set it down in front of her daughter who screwed up her face and began to whine:

—But I wanted to put in the sugar BY MYSELF!

—Next time, okay? Tomorrow.

—But this is tomorrow. THIS IS TOMORROW!

—This is today. The day you're on is always today.

It is not! Don't you dare say that! said the child. The bottom lip was pushed out and a couple of large tears pooled in the corners of her angry eyes. The baby laughed and banged the table with a chubby fist.

—It's not funny, said her big sister.

—She's just trying to cheer you up, said her mother.

—She's not! But anyway anyway anyway how can I cheer up when I've just been upset.

151

As the baby girned in response to her sister's sudden gush of tears, the toast began to smoke under the grill but the mother turned it over anyway, poured boiling water into her baby's mush and—to avoid lumps and choking fits—stirred as patiently as she could. She fetched a couple of rattles from the toybox and put them in front of the wee one to keep her occupied while the food cooled. She made coffee, took the toast out from under the grill, spread it with butter and bit off a large chunk. Her daughter was dragging her spoon through the porridge, turning what had been a fairly appetising plateful into a lumpy, sloshing mess. She had not yet begun to eat. The baby was hitting itself in the face with a rattle. The mush was still too hot for the baby so the mother finished her toast, gulped down a mouthful of coffee, walked briskly through to the bedroom and shook, gently, the exposed shoulder of her husband. She shook the shoulder again, firmly. She announced the time then went back to the kitchen.

Five minutes later, after managing to aim a few mouthfuls of food into the baby's roaming mouth, she returned to the bedroom and went through the shaking-waking process again. This time she was shrill. Her husband's eyes and mouth opened suddenly, as if she had dunted his skull with a mallet. His body jerked into a sitting position, then slumped back against the pillow.

—What day is it?

—My day, said the mother. My day away.

—Right, said the husband. Right. He shook himself and rolled out of bed.

Back in the kitchen the mother said:

—You haven't touched your porridge.

—My spoon has, said her daughter. You've got a dress on.

—Eat up now.

—You've got a dress on. Why have you got a dress on?

—Yes, I've got a dress on.

—Are you going to a party? Can I come too? Can I wear my party dress and my tights with the Silver Minnie Mouses on the legs?

—It's nursery today. I'm not going to a party. I'm going to a conference. Cold porridge tastes horrible, you know.

—You know, this porridge tastes horrible and it's not even cold. HA HA HA HA. What's a confrence?

—Eat up now.

—What's a confrence?

—A kind of meeting. Lots of people meet and talk. I have to stand up and talk. About children. You don't want me to tell them that my little girl doesn't eat her porridge? Slowly her daughter raised a loaded spoon to her mouth and turned suspicious eyes on her mother.

—Are the people strangers?

—Most of them will be.

—I'm not allowed to talk to strangers. Why are you going to talk to strangers?

—I'll tell you tomorrow, said the mother.

—But this is tomorrow! You said last night you were going away tomorrow!

Dilys Rose (b. 1954)
Red Tides, Minerva (1993)

To make porridge

4 Servings

Put 2 pts/1 1/4 litres water (5c) into a pot and bring to the boil. Sprinkle in 4oz/125g medium oatmeal (1c) with one hand, while stirring with a spurtle (long wooden stick) to prevent lumps forming. Lower the heat, cover and leave to simmer for anything up to 30 minutes.

It does reduce and thicken so it is very much a case of how thick you like it. Some prefer it cooked for a shorter rather than a longer time, about five minutes (In which case, reduce water by half). Apart from saving time, it is less jelly-like in texture and the grains still have some bite to them.

Season with a generous pinch of salt and serve in bowls with a smaller bowl of milk, cream or buttermilk. Natural yoghurt, especially the Greek variety made from ewes' milk is good with porridge and even better with a spoonful of molasses on top.

Catherine Brown
Scottish Cookery, Richard Drew (1986)

Mercat

And richt by the factory waa, the first ferm,
The couthie country fat and fou o ferms
As far as the legend-land of Foggieloan,
Ayont the trees whas line alang the lift
Aince gart a bairn believe the mairch of the warld
Fand endin thonder, aye the warld gaes yokan,
Wi park on park for the plou,
Park on park for the paidle,
Parks for the beasts and parks for the barley
(The meat and the meal and the bree of the barley —
Aye, aye, the haill hypothec),
And aa for the mercat, aa for the Friday mart,
The fermers fat as their ferms,
Braid as their beasts and bauld as their barley-bree,
Come traikan intil the toun to swap their trauchle,
To niffer for nowt at the unco unction,
Yarkan their bids as the yammeran unctioneer,
And syne frae the pens til the pubs whaur business is
        pleisure,
To slocken the stour frae thrang thrapples
In whacks of whisky and lochans o lowse ale
Whaur aa the clash o the country roun gaes sooman,
Skyrie wi mauts and skinklan-bricht wi beers
That wash the langour awa frae the landwart week,
Their trinkle the toun's freedom for ilka fermer.

Alexander Scott (1920-89)
'Heart of Stone' (1965)
Collected Poems, Mercat Press (1994)

An Antiquary's Dinner

The dinner was such as suited a professed antiquary, comprehending many savoury specimens of Scottish viands, now disused at tables of those who affect elegance. There was the relishing Solan goose, whose smell is so powerful that he is never cooked within the house. Blood-raw he proved to be on this occasion, so that Mr Oldbuck half-threatened to throw the greasy sea-fowl at the head of the negligent housekeeper, who acted as priestess in presenting this odoriferous offering. But by good-hap, she had been most fortunate in the hotch-potch, which was unanimously pronounced to be inimitable. "I knew we should succeed here," said Oldbuck exultingly, "for Davie Dibble, the gardener (an old bachelor like myself), takes care the rascally women do not dishonour our vegetables. And here is fish and sauce, and crappit heads—I acknowledge our womankind excel in that dish—it procures them the pleasure of scolding, for half an hour at least, twice a week, with auld Maggie Mucklebackit, our fish-wife. The chicken-pie, Mr Lovel, is made after a recipe bequeathed to me by my departed grandmother of happy memory. —And if you will venture on a glass of wine, you will find it worthy of one who professes the maxim of King Alphonso of Castile— old wood to burn—old books to read—old wine to drink—and old friends, Sir Arthur—ay, Mr Lovel, and young friends too, to converse with."

Sir Walter Scott
The Antiquary, Constable (1816)

The Grand Feast

"And who gave you leave to invite company into your grandmama's house?" cried Mrs Crabtree, snatching up all the notes, and angrily thrusting them into the fire. "I never heard of such doings in all my life before, Master Harry! but as sure as eggs are eggs, you shall repent of this, for not one morsel of cake or anything else shall you give to any of the party; no! not as much as a crust of bread, or a thimbleful of tea!"

Harry and Laura had never thought of such a catastrophe as this before; they always saw a great table covered with everything that could be named for tea, whenever any little friends came to visit them; and whether it rose out of the floor, or was brought by Aladdin's lamp, they never considered it possible that the table would not be provided as usual on such occasions; so this terrible speech of Mrs Crabtree's frightened them out of their wits. What was to be done! They both knew by experience that she always did what she threatened or something a great deal worse, so they began by bursting into tears, and begging Mrs Crabtree for this once to excuse them, and to give some cakes and tea to their little visitors; but they might as well have spoken to one of the Chinese mandarins, for she only shook her head with a positive look, declaring over and over and over again that nothing should appear upon the table except what was always brought up for their own supper— two biscuits and two cups of milk.

"Therefore say no more about it!" added she, sternly. "I am your best friend, Master Harry, trying to teach you and Miss Laura your duty; so save your breath to cool your porridge."

Poor Harry and Laura looked perfectly ill with fright and vexation when they thought of what was to happen next, while Mrs Crabtree sat down to her knitting, grumbling to herself, and dropping her stitches every minute, with rage. Old Andrew felt exceedingly sorry after he heard what distress and difficulty Harry was in; and when the hour for the party approached, he very good-naturedly spread out a large table in the dining-room, where he put down as many cups, saucers, plates and spoons, as Laura chose; but in spite of all his trouble, though it looked very grand, there was nothing whatever to eat or drink except the two dry biscuits, and the two miserable cups of milk, which seemed to become smaller every time that Harry looked at them.

Presently the clock struck six, and Harry listened to the hour very much as a prisoner would do in the condemned cell in Newgate, feeling that the dreaded time was at last arrived. Soon afterwards several handsome carriages drove up to the door, filled with little Masters and Misses, who hurried joyfully into the house, talking and laughing all the way up stairs, while poor Harry and Laura almost wished the floor would open and swallow them up; so they shrunk into a distant corner of the room, quite ashamed to show their faces.

The young ladies were all dressed in their best frocks, with pink sashes, and white shoes: while the little boys appeared in their holiday clothes, with their hair newly brushed, and their faces washed. The whole party had dined at two o' clock, so they were as hungry as hawks, looking eagerly round, whenever they entered, to see what was on the tea-table, and evidently surprised that nothing had yet been put down. Laura and Harry soon afterwards heard their visitors whispering to each other about Norwich buns, rice-cakes, sponge biscuits, and macaroons; while Peter Grey was loud in praise of a party at George Lorraine's the night before, when an immense plum-cake had been sugared over like a snow storm, and covered with crowds of beautiful amusing mottoes; not to mention a quantity of noisy crackers, that exploded like pistols; besides which, a glass of hot jelly had been handed to each little guest before he was sent home.

Every time the door opened, all eyes were anxiously turned round, expecting a grand feast to be brought in; but quite the contrary—it was only Andrew showing up more hungry visitors; while Harry felt so unspeakably wretched, that, if some kind fairy could only have turned him into a Norwich bun at the moment, he would gladly have consented to be cut in pieces, that his ravenous guests might be satisfied.

Catherine Sinclair (1800-64)
Holiday House: A Book for the Young (1856)

Alexander Smith

A Skye Kitchen

The shepherds, the shepherds' dogs, and the domestic servants, dined in the large kitchen. The kitchen was the most picturesque apartment in the house. There was a huge dresser near the small dusty window; in a dark corner stood a great cupboard in which crockery was stowed away. The walls and rafters were black with peat smoke. Dogs were continually sleeping on the floor with their heads resting on their outstretched paws; and from a frequent start and whine, you knew that in dream they were chasing a flock of sheep along the steep hill-side, their masters shouting out orders to them from the valley beneath. The fleeces of sheep which had been found dead on the mountain were nailed on the walls to dry. Braxy hams were suspended from the roof; strings of fish were hanging above the fire-place. The door was almost continually open, for by the door light mainly entered. Amid a savoury steam of broth and potatoes, the shepherds and domestic servants drew in long backless forms to the table, and dined, innocent of knife and fork, the dogs snapping and snarling among their legs; and when the meal was over, the dogs licked the platters. Macara, who was something of a poet, would, on his occasional visits, translate Gaelic poems for me. On one occasion, after one of these translations had been read, I made the remark that a similar set of ideas occurred in one of the songs of Burns. His gray eyes immediately blazed up; he rushed into a Gaelic recitation of considerable length; and, at its close, snapping defiant fingers in my face, demanded, "Can you produce anything out of your Shakespeare or your Burns equal to *that*? Of course, I could not; and I fear I aggravated my original offence by suggesting that in all likelihood my main inability to produce a passage of corresponding excellence from the southern authors arose from my entire ignorance of the language of the native bard. When Peter came with his violin, the kitchen was cleared after nightfall; the forms were taken away, candles stuck into the battered tin sconces, the dogs unceremoniously kicked out, and a somewhat ample ball room was the result.

Alexander Smith (1830-67)
A Summer in Skye, Strahan (1865)

Gaelic Stories

(5)
Croit.
Dà bhràthair.
Truinnsear le buntàta

(5)
A croft
Two brothers.
A plate with potatoes.

(9)
"Romance"
eadar càis
is bainne.

(9)
A romance
between cheese
and milk.

(14)
Còmhradh
eadar lof is
mulachag.

(14)
A conversation
between a loaf and
cheese.

(15)
Còmhradh
eadar bòtann
is sgadan

(15)
A conversation
between a wellington
and a herring.

(16)
Còmhradh
eadar ìm ùr
is copan.

(16)
A conversation
between fresh butter
and a cup.

Iain Crichton Smith (b. 1928)
Eadar Fealla-dha Is Glaschu (Glasgow 1974)
Selected Poems 1955-1980

Tobias Smollett

A Hunting Breakfast

This morning we got up by four, to hunt the roebuck, and, in an half an hour, found breakfast ready served in the hall. . . . The following articles formed our morning's repast: one kit of boiled eggs; a second, full of butter; a third, full of cream; an entire cheese, made of goat's milk; a large earthen pot full of honey; the best part of a ham; a cold venison pasty; a bushel of oatmeal, made in thin cakes and bannocks, with a small wheaten loaf in the middle for the strangers; a large stone bottle full of whisky, another of brandy, and a kilderkin of ale. There was a ladle chained to the cream kit, with curious wooden bickers to be filled from this reservoir. The spirits were drunk out of a silver quaff, and the ale out of horns: great justice was done to the collation by the guests in general; one of them in particular ate above two dozen of hard eggs, with a proportionable quantity of bread, butter, and honey; nor was one drop of liquor left upon the board. Finally, a large roll of tabacco was presented by way of dessert, and every individual took a comfortable quid, to prevent the bad effects of the morning air. . . .

Haggis and Oatcakes

Now we are upon the article of cookery, I must own, some of their dishes are savoury, and even delicate; but I am not yet Scotchman enough to relish their singed sheep's head and haggis, which were provided, at our request, one day at Mr Mitchelson's, where we dined. The first put me in mind of the history of the Congo, in which I had read of negroes' head sold publiciy in the markets; the last, being a mess of minced lights, livers, suet, oatmeal, onions, and pepper, enclosed in a sheep's stomach, had a very sudden effect upon mine, and the delicate Mrs Tabby changed colour; when the cause of our disgust was instantaneously removed at the nod of our entertainer. The Scotch in general are attached to this composition with a sort of national fondness, as well as to their oatmeal bread; which is presented at every table, in thin triangular cakes, baked up on a plate of iron, called a girdle; and these many of the natives, even in the higher ranks of life, prefer to wheaten bread, which they have here in perfection.

Tobias Smollett (1721-71)
The Expedition of Humphry Clinker (1771)

Blaeberry Mou

The flitterin faces come doun the brae
And the baskets gowd and green;
And nane but a blindie wud speer the day
Whaur a' the bairns hae been.

The life is blue, and the hills are blue,
And the lochan in atween;
But nane sae blue as the blaeberry mou'
That needna tell whaur it's been.

William Soutar (1898-1945)
Poems in Scots and English, SAP (1975)

Supper

Steepies for the bairnie
Sae moolie in the mou':
Parritch for a strappan lad
To mak his beard grow.

Stovies for a muckle man
To keep him stout and hale:
A noggin for the auld carl
To gar him sleep weel.

Bless the meat, and bless the drink,
And the hand that steers the pat:
And be guid to beggar-bodies
Whan they come to your yett.

William Soutar (1898-1945)
Collected Poems, Andrew Dakars (1948)

Stonehaven Haddocks

Friday, August 27—

At tea last night, and at breakfast this morning we had Findon haddocks, which Mr Telford would not allow us to taste at Dundee, not till we reached Stonehaven, lest this boasted dainty of Aberdeen should be disparaged by a bad specimen. The fish is very slightly salted, and as slightly smoked by a peat fire, after which the sooner they are eaten the better. They are said to be in the market (for the most part) twelve hours after they have been caught, and longer than twenty four they ought not to be kept. They are broiled, or toasted, I know not which; and are as good as any fish of little flavour can be when thus cured. The haddocks of this coast are smaller than those which are brought to London, or to Dublin, and better; but at the best it is a poor fish, a little less insipid than cod.

Robert Southey (1774-1843)
Journal of a Tour in Scotland in 1819
ed. C. H. Hereford, John Murray (1929)

"In Scotland I have eaten nettles, I have slept in nettle sheets and I have dined off a nettle tablecloth. . . . The stalks of the old nettles are as good as flax for making cloth. I have heard my mother say that she thought nettle cloth more durable than any other species of linen."

Thomas Campbell (1777-1844)

Muriel Spark

Pineapple Cubes

Sandy Stranger had a feeling at the time that they were supposed to be the happiest days of her life, and on her tenth birthday she said so to her best friend Jenny Gray who had been asked to tea at Sandy's house. The speciality of the feast was pineapple cubes with cream, and the speciality of the day was that they were left to themselves. To Sandy the unfamiliar pineapple had the authentic taste and appearance of happiness and she focussed her small eyes closely on the pale gold cubes before she scooped them up in her spoon, and she thought the sharp taste on her tongue was that of a special happiness, which was nothing to do with eating, and was different from the happiness of play that one enjoyed unawares. Both girls saved the cream to last, then ate it in spoonfuls.

"Little girls, you are going to be the crème de la crème," said Sandy, and Jenny spluttered her cream into her handkerchief.

"You know," Sandy said, "these are supposed to be the happiest days of our lives."

"Yes, they are always saying that," Jenny said. "They say, make the most of your schooldays because you never know what lies ahead of you."

Muriel Spark (b. 1918)
The Prime of Miss Jean Brodie, Macmillan (1961)

Limpets

The time I spent upon the island is still so horrible a thought to me, that I must pass it lightly over. In all the books I have read of people cast away, they had either their pocket full of tools, or a chest of things would be thrown upon the beach along with them, as if on purpose. My case was very different. I had nothing in my pockets but money and Alan's silver button; and being inland bred, I was as much short of knowledge as of means.

I knew indeed that shell-fish were counted good to eat; and among the rocks of the isle I found a great plenty of limpets, which at first I could scarcely strike from their places, not knowing quickness to be needful. There were, besides, some of the little shells that we call buckies; I think periwinkle is the English name. Of these two I made my whole diet devouring them cold and raw as I found them; and so hungry was I, that at first they seemed to me delicious.

Perhaps they were out of season, or perhaps there was something wrong in the sea about my island. But at least I had no sooner eaten my first meal than I was seized with a giddiness and retching, and lay for a long time no better than dead. A second trial of the food (indeed I had no other) did better with me and revived my strength. But as long as I was on the Island, I never knew what to expect when I had eaten; sometimes all was well and sometimes I was thrown into a miserable sickness; nor could I ever distinguish what particular fish it was that hurt me.

R L Stevenson (1850-94)
Kidnapped Cassell, (1886)

Robert Louis Stevenson

Lord Hermiston's Dinners

When things went wrong at dinner, as they continually did, my lord would look up the table at his wife: "I think thees broth would be better to sweem in than to sup." Or else talk to the butler: "Here, M'Killop, awa' wi' this Raadical gigot—tak' it to the French man, and bring me some puddocks! It seems rather a sore kind of business that I should be all day in Court hanging Raadicals, and get nawthing to my dinner." Of course, this was but a manner of speaking and he had never hanged a man for being a Radical in his life; the law, of which he was the faithful minister, directing otherwise. And of course these growls were in the nature of pleasantry, but it was of a recondite sort; and uttered as they were in his resounding voice, and commented on by that expression which they called in the Parliament House 'Hermiston's hanging face'— they struck mere dismay into the wife.

She sat before him speechless and fluttering; at each dish, as at a fresh ordeal, her eye hovered towards my lord's countenance and fell again; if he but ate in silence, unspeakable relief was her portion; if there were complaint, the world was darkened. She would seek out the cook, who was always her *sister in the Lord*. "O my dear, this is the most dreidful thing that my lord can never be contented in his own house!" she would begin; and weep and pray with the cook; and then the cook would pray with Mrs Weir; and the next day's meal would be never a penny the better—and the next cook (when she came) would be worse if anything, but just as pious. It was often wondered that Lord Hermiston bore it as he did; indeed he was a stoical old voluptuary, contented with sound wine and plenty of it. But there were moments when he overflowed. Perhaps half a dozen times in the history of his married life—"Here! tak' it awa', and bring me a piece of bread and kebbuck!" he had exclaimed, with an appalling explosion of his voice and rare gestures. None thought to dispute or to make excuses; the service was arrested; Mrs Weir sat at the head of the table whimpering without disguise; and his lordship opposite munched his bread and cheese in ostentatious disregard. Only once Mrs Weir had ventured to appeal. He was passing her chair on his way in to the study.

"O, Edom!" she wailed, in a voice tragic with tears, and reaching out to him both hands, in one of which she held a sopping pocket-handkerchief.

He paused, and looked upon her with a face of wrath, into which there stole, as he looked, a twinkle of humour.

"Noansense!" he said. "You and your noansense! What do I want with a Christian faim'ly? I want Christian broth! Get me a lass that can plain-boil a potato, if she was a whüre off the streets."

Robert Louis Stevenson
Weir of Hermiston, Chatto & Windus(1896)

Very early in the spring, long before the cold east winds of March have gone, the women take up their positions. Each one has an improvised table, consisting frequently of an orange box, on which are placed saucers containing shellfish, together with the necessary condiments.

J. H. Jamieson
'The Edinburgh Street Traders and their Cries' in the
Book of the Old Edinburgh Club (1909)

John Strang

The Duck Club of Partick

It was about the period when Partick was in its more rural condition, that there existed divers knots of individuals connected with Glasgow, who, inspired by the noble purpose of enjoying ducks and green peas in perfection, with cold punch in ditto, proceeded hebdomadally to indulge their gastronomic propensities at this picturesque village. Among the many inducements which this locality offered to these united bands of kindred spirits were, the agreeable health-inspiring distance of this common rendezvous from the smoky City—the picturesque appearance of the village itself—the refreshing flow of the limpid Kelvin, broken by successive cascades—the neat and comfortable character of the hostelry; and, above all, the superior quality of ducks reared under all the known advantages that arise from the proximity which large grain-mills naturally afford for good feeding. To these inducements, too, was super-added the delicious manner in which the ducks were prepared for table, and which never failed to excite an appetite, which was only appeased after each guest had finished his bird!

[Of the Convener of the Partick Duck Club] the Club poet, Mr William Reid . . . improvised the following true and touching couplet:

> "The ducks at Partick quack for fear,
> Crying, 'Lord preserve us! there's McTear!' "

And no wonder. For no sooner was the rubicund beak of the worthy Convener espied by the blue and white swimmers of the mill-dam, than it was certain that the fate of those now disporting would become, ere another Saturday, that of their jolly companions who at that moment were suffering martyrdom at the *auto-da-fe* in the kitchen of the 'Bunhouse'! Though the ducks, as may reasonably be supposed, quacked loudly in anticipation of their coming fate, yet the Convener, having no sympathy with anything akin to the melting mood, except what was produced by the sun's summer beams, was deaf to pity. He felt too strongly the truth of Cato's famous saying that 'it is no easy task to preach to the belly, which has no ears'. The truth is, that neither the poetry of Reid nor the quacking of the ducks had any power over the alimentative bump of the carnivorous Convener. Its cry never ceased from June till October, when, alas! the broad sheet of water which, in spring, had been almost covered with the feathered flock of youthful divers, was found, in autumn, altogether untenanted, save by the few lamenting parents of their once happy and noisy families! The Convener and the Club had during the summer's campaign, made conscripts of all the young, and had sacrificed them to their own gustative propensities, without one *tear* for the family bereavements they were meekly occasioning, except, perhaps, when that was now and then called forth through the pungency of the *spiritual* consolation which universally followed the Saturday holocaust.

And, in good troth, when we reflect on those duck feasts, we do not wonder at the weekly turn out of guests who congregated at Partick, or that there should have been, in consequence, a hebdomadal murder of the innocents to meet the craving of the Club. For we verily believe, that never did even the all-famous *'Trois frères Provenceaux'*, in the Palais Royal at Paris, send up from their celebrated *cuisine*, a *canard roti* in better style than did the landlady of the Partick 'Bunhouse' her roasted duck, done to a turn and redolent with sage and onion;—and then the peas, all green and succulent, and altogether free from the mint of England and the sugar of France! What a glorious sight it was to see the Club met, and what a subject would such a meeting have afforded to the pointer of character and manners! The rosy countenance and bold bearing of the president, seated at the head of a table surrounded by at least a dozen of happy guests almost as rubicund and sleek as himself, each grinning with cormorant eye over his smoking duckling, and only waiting the short interval of a hastily muttered grace to plant his ready knife into its full and virgin bosom;—verily, the spectacle must have been a cheering one!

John Strang (1795-1863)
Glasgow and its Clubs, Richard Griffin (1856)

Emma Tennant

Pies and Hardboiled Eggs

My mother called to me from the kitchen to come in. It was the summer holidays: long, empty, grey days. Today the jeep would come along the mud track, over the top of the hill, and the laird and his party would spread rugs out in front of our cottage, on the sloping grass by the overflowing burn. In the gentle rain, watched by sheep, they would eat pies and hardboiled eggs and drink beer and wine, leaving the cans and bottles for my mother to collect. Then, flushed, they would go slowly up the hills to their holes. I was never allowed to be there. But if the daughter was with them she would twist on her rug and gaze at the windows of the house. Her mother, fair-haired as her daughter, and self-contained, also with an expression of secret amusement on her face most of the time, never turned to look at the cottage. When she walked back to the jeep with the picnic basket after lunch, it was always head down, eyes on the thin grass by the track and the sheep droppings, and the ugly colt's foot that grew there, yellow and darkened with rain.

Emma Tennant (b. 1938)
The Bad Sister, Gollancz (1978)

Derick Thomson

Lus a' Chorracha-mille

Tha a' chlann a' tional lus a' chorracha-mille
faisg air a' chreig, air slios a' ghlinne,
a' cladhach nam freumhaichean fada geala,
's a' caomhnadh nan cnapan milis meala;
cnothan a' gheamhraidh, a ghleidheas am milseachd
ged tha 'n talamh fuar 's an duilleag air crìonadh.

Thionail mis' uair lus a' chorracha-mille—
mil air do bheul, mil air do shùgradh;
cha b'ann air aodann na creige, no slios a' ghlinne—
mil air do bheul, mil mhilis do chùill-sa;
cha do shail mi gun mharbh mi na cnothan, ged rinn mi an
                                                        tìoradh,
cha do shail mi gun chiall mi a' mhil, ged a rinn mu a sìoladh,
cha do shail mi gun dh'fhalbh an uraidh ged thàinig am blianna.

Is thionail mise uair eile lus a' chorracha-mille,
sgrìob is ghlan mi na cnothan, is chuir mi air falbh iad,
an àite dìomhair dorch, an cùil na cuimhne,
air chùl a' mheadhail, an taigh an aoibhneis,
far nach fhaiceadh sùil is nach blaiseadh beul orr',
ann an taigh a' mheadhail, air chùl an èibhneis.
Lus a' chorracha-mille a mhill mo shuaimhneas,
bu chorrach do chìoch, 's a' mhil a' sruthadh uaipe,
ged nach do ràinig orm-s' ach deireadh druaip dhith.

(trans. overpage)

Derick Thomson

Wild Liquorice

The children are gathering the wild liquorice
close to the rocks, on the side of the glen,
digging up the long white roots
and saving the honey-sweet nodules;
winter nuts that keep their sweetness
though the ground is cold and the leaf shrivelled.

Once upon a time I gathered wild liquorice —
honey on your lips, honey on your love-talk;
not on the rock-face, nor the glen-side —
honey on your lips, sweet honey of your music;
I did not think the nuts had died though I dried them out,
nor that I had lost the honey, though I filtered it,
nor that last year was gone though this year came.

And another time, I gathered wild liquorice,
scraped and cleaned the nuts and put them away,
in a dark secret place, in a nook in the memory,
behind mirth in the house of joy,
where eye could not see, nor lips taste,
in the house of mirth, behind joy.
Wild liquorice that wiled my peace,
with honey flowing from the point of your breast,
though all that reached me was the very last drop.

Derick Thomson
Creachadh na Clàrsaich/Plundering the Harp, MacDonald (1982)

Tony

Tony Jaconelli, Mediterranean man
In our rainy little west of Scotland town,
Dispensed Italian ice-cream, white and sweet.
Big cones, bloodied with raspberry juice
Stuck magically in his brown left hand.
'Ica-creema, coolla-bella! For you and you!'
He trilled in strange un-Scottish English.

'Only after your pennies,' our dour elders
Would mutter, but smiles and songs dropped
From his lips like tendrils of spaghetti:
We had our money's worth twice over
At every exotic ceremony.

The war changed things. We heard odd words at home
As we chewed our stodgy Scottish tea-bread —
'Internment—enemy alien—fascist pig!
Mussolini's chin provoked our beery patriots
To boycott Tony's place and smash his windows
Till soldiers took him away for the duration.
'For his own good,' so every body said.

When he came back in forty-six, old and grey,
The smiles and songs had gone forever.

Geddes Thomson (b. 1939)
Four Scottish Poets, Garron Press (1982)

Valerie Thornton

Dumpling and Lucky Potatoes

Jim has brought some dumpling, he said, there's a piece for you too.

Dumpling. The stuff you get in the butcher, shiny brown slices with liberal quantities of the little black currants, hard and burnt tasting, sometimes with nasty little crunchy bits of stem or pip left in. Dumplings which the butcher gathers with hands bloody from mince and livers. He slaps the slices on the weighing machine's splattered surface and wraps them up with the raw sausages. Sometimes there's little red bits clinging to the cooked dumpling which you have to pick off. Dumpling with plastic round the outside, which you grill with the sausage and black budding and which always burns hard and dry. The only dumpling now.

His mum made it for his father's birthday or something, he adds.

A vague memory stirs, but you let it rest.

Until you feel peckish and wander through to the kitchen. The dumpling's in the cupboard, wrapped in an opaque polythene bag, hidden from the cats. As soon as you open the bag, the smell seduces you, melts the years, dissolves the present. A smell unknown for what— you stop to count—ten, maybe twenty, years?

The mixed spices rise warm and friendly. The sultanas gleam quietly in the soft brown mixture of dried fruits and orange peel, flattened moon slices encircled by that wonderful thing—the skin of a clootie dumpling.

You loved them then. This one, Jim's Mum's one, is good. But it is only the key to the memory of heavenly ones.

When it was drawing near your birthday, you would ask Mrs MacDougall please to make you a dumpling. And she would give your mother a list of things she needed because your mother never kept them in the house. Mixed spices—cinnamon, ginger and nutmeg, lots of sultanas, a bag of flour, a red, blue and yellow box of suet, and maybe other things. Little silver secrets, wrapped in greaseproof paper and hidden in the mixture—a thimble for an old maid, a horseshoe for luck, a ring for a wedding, a coin for wealth.

Mrs MacDougall would swing out the kitchen table with the red formica top into the middle of the room and put up the leaf so that she had room to work, with her sleeves rolled up, beating and mixing, raising a spicy cloud around her.

A clean linen dishcloth would be waiting nearby, the fine white kind with the blue or red borders. If you weren't already there, Mrs MacDougall would call you down when the bowl was ready to lick, when the mixture was tied up in the towel and simmering in a pan on the cooker. It would cook for hours, for all the morning, while Mrs MacDougall cleaned and ironed and washed and tidied and told you things.

She used to take your old bread for the hens. The hens were up on the wasteground beside her mother's house. Then when they built houses there, and the hens went away, she still took the bread. But she would bring potted hough which she made herself for you. And always she would make a big pot of soup for the weekend, and wash and peel all the vegetables and leave them on top of the washing machine in a big bowl of water. She was so fast at peeling potatoes. You would stand by her elbow and watch her hand whizzing round a potato so fast you could hardly follow it. Then she would fish in the basin of cold water, thick with skin and earth, and bring out another dark potato to peel. You would talk about lucky potatoes, which she too remembered buying when she was little. Sweet cinnamon-dusted slices of delicious crumbly white stuff, with a gift concealed in it. She used to get silver threepennies when she was little, but now you get plastic soldiers or aeroplanes. You have to lick and suck and poke the sweet potato out of the tiny spaces on the gift.

She never eats sweets herself now; she used to ice cakes in a baker's shop and that put her off for life. But she likes pepper. She loves to see your face when she tells you she gets through a carton of pepper a week. And just to prove it, she always puts pepper on her cheese sandwich for elevenses.

Valerie Thornton (b. 1954)
'Only This' *New Writing Scotland 5,* ASLS (1987)

Edinburgh Suppers

When dinners are given here, they are invitations of form. The entertainment of pleasure is their suppers, which resemble the *petit soupers* of France. Of these they are very fond; and it is a mark of their friendship to be admitted to be of the party. It is in these meetings that the pleasures of society and conversation reign, when restraints of ceremony are banished, and you see people really as they are: and I must say, in honour of the Scotch, that I never met with a more agreeable people, with more pleasing or more insinuating manners, in my life. These little parties generally consist of about seven or eight persons, which prevents the conversation from being particular, and which it always must be in larger companies. During the supper, which continues some time, the Scotch Ladies drink more wine than an English woman could well bear; but the climate requires it, and probably in some measure it may enliven their natural vivacity.

Edward Topham (1751-1820)
Letters from Edinburgh 1774-1775 (1776)

That's Hotch-Potch—and that's cocky-leeky—the twa best soups in natur. Broon soup's moss-water—and white soup's like scauded milk wi' worms in't. But see, sirs, hoo the ladle stauns o' itsel in the potch. . . .

Christopher North

176

A Scottish Breakfast

A good dish of fish, often of mixed fish, fresh out of the water, could be had for a shilling in those days. Oysters were a shilling the 'half-thunder.' Think of it, gourmand! Half-a-hundred fine, delicately-flavoured Firth of Forth oysters, for a paltry shilling—and the bell-like tones of 'Caller oo!' filling the outer air with melody, thrown into the bargain!

If my two Colquhoun uncles were coming to breakfast any day, fish was always provided, as sea-fish was an agreeable change from the trout, perch and 'powan' of Loch Lomond. Why they should have cared to walk down from Edinburgh, where they would be located at the time, to *breakfast*, instead of to some more reasonable meal, one wonders; but it may have been that the fashion set in London by Rogers, and his contemporary wits and poets, had permeated other kinds of society.

Anyhow, they came; when I was old enough to remember, they had long got into the habit of coming every now and again; and though my parents kept very early hours—from choice, for they were among those who, having nothing to do, had all day to do it in—there was no change made for the guest.

Who that knows a Scottish breakfast will not confess that it is hard to beat? I can see my parent's breakfast-table yet: the many varied dishes, hot and cold; the dark and light jellies—(black currant and white currant—what has become of white currant jelly?—one never sees it now); then such potato scones, barley scones and scones that were just 'scones' and nothing else, each kind nicely wrapped up in its snowy napkin, with the little peak that lifted and fell back, falling lower and lower as the pile diminished; the brown eggs that everyone prefers to white—and why?—the butter, the sweet, old yellow butter, framed in watercress. It does not seem strange, all things considered, that the two bachelors who appeared at half-past eight o' clock on the door-step of their brother's house found it worth their while to bring to the long, leisurely meal before them sharpened appetites and pleasantly tired limbs.

Lucy Bethia Walford (1845-1915)

Braxy

Owing to improvidence or ill-luck, no food had been tasted by any of the party since an early breakfast; wherefore it may be imagined how appetising would have been the odour of frizzling trout, or savoury ham and eggs, or in short, almost anything that might have seemed within the range of the solitary inn.

Almost anything? Certainly anything in the shape of buffalo steak, or rhinoceros hump. We sat round the crackling fire in the little peat-reeking parlour, and cheerfully awaited our supper. Whatever it might consist of, we were, or thought we were, prepared for it.

But *braxy mutton*? Has the reader ever tasted, has he ever smelt, braxy mutton? Mutton so called is the body of a sheep which has either died, or had to be killed, when suffering from a complaint which, though hard upon the sheep, is innocuous to the eater. The sheep, having reached an advanced state of *embonpoint*, surrenders to fate, and this mutton is largely consumed, and not at all objected to, by the denizens of the Scottish wilds.

But oh, that first whiff from the kitchen! That puff from the passage! Our sickened stomachs could stand no more; and as the horrible dish was borne in, with one accord we demanded that it should be borne out again.

We tried the eggs. Another anguish of disappointment.

Then the scones. They were damp, flabby, and tough beyond power of thought to conceive: teeth could not rend them.

Lastly cakes (bread there was none); and the oatcakes, hard as flint, dry, tasteless, and white as a dusty road in a March east wind, proved the only accompaniment to the hot whisky-toddy which helped us to endure starvation.

Lucy Bethia Walford (1845-1915)
Recollections of a Scottish Novelist, Kylin Press (1984)

Escape from the City of Gold

I remember the drabness of Heathrow, followed by the depressing connecting flight north of the border. We were all fucked anyway after the long journey from Johannesburg, but they had cancelled a couple of planes because of ice on the runway. London was freezing; Scotland would be even worse. It shows how dense and in a world of my own I had been eighteen months before, because I had been almost as excited that we were stopping off in London as I was that we were on our way to Johannesburg. I thought of London as somewhere just as distant and exotic; I had been surprised on the outward journey when we arrived there so quickly. Returning though, I saw London for what it was: the grizzled fag-end of the British Islands.

On our last day, I'd had to say goodbye to my friends at school and to my teachers. It was strange, but I seemed to be popular there; a big cheese, a top boy, numero uno. My best pals were called Pieter and Curtis. I was a bit of a bully to Curtis. Pieter was too. He was quite a wild cunt and was well pissed off that I was going back. It was good to have someone miss you. Most of the other kids were a bit slow and sappy. I would miss Pieter but, as this was the first time I'd discovered that I had a brain, the person I would miss most was Miss Carvello, one of my teachers. She was beautiful, with big, dark eyes. I used to wank about her, my first real wank, like, when you get spunk. She told Vet it was fortunate that I was leaving South Africa as I had come on leaps and bounds at school and was 'university material'. This unfortunate phrase was to be thrown back at me in all my subsequent under-achievement.

I wanted to stay in South Africa. What I had gained there was a perverse sense of empowerment; an ego even. I knew I was fuckin special, whatever any of them tried to tell me. I knew I wasn't going to be like the rest of them; my old man, my old lady, Bernard, Tony, Kim, the other kids back in the scheme. They were rubbish. They were nothing. I was Roy Strang. Maybe I had to go back, but it was going to be different. I wasnae gaunna take any shite.

Back in Scotland, when John finally came home, we had a family meal to celebrate. Everyone was there, not quite everyone, Winston Two being back in quarantine, and Elgin still at THE GORGIE VENTURE

FOR EXCEPTIONAL YOUNG MEN. It was considered too off-putting to have him home at the dinnertable, and I confess that I had been one of the principal advocates of keeping him away. Only Kim, Vet and Bernard argued for his presence, but John, as always, had the last word. —It widnae be fair tae the laddie, disorientate um, like ah sais, disorientate um.

The dinner was excellent. Ma made broth, then spaghetti carbonara with sprouts, broccoli and roast tatties heaped on top so as you could hardly see the pasta or the sauce, followed by sherry trifle. The bottles of Liebfraumilch were heartily drained. I'd never seen a table so loaded with food. We seldom ate around the table as a family, generally balancing plates on our laps as we jostled for position around the telly. This, we were told, was a special occasion.

There was, however, a tense atmosphere in the house at the meal; Tony's face was heavy with sweat as he ploughed into the food, while Kim pushed hers around. Bernard had a violent argument with John earlier and instead of sitting down had sort of collapsed into the chair, ashen-faced and trembling. He was trying to cut a piece of roast tattie, his breath making high little sounds which could have come from the throat of a dog. Later on Kim was to tell me that Dad had heard from Mum about something Bernard had done with another laddie and had threatened to cut his cock off.

Mum and Dad had obviously argued about it and were both wound up so tightly as they sat at the table that the air around them seemed to gel. I ate nervously and quickly, anxious to excuse myself, feeling that one wrong word of dubious gesture might spark off a massacre.

—These tatties are hoat . . . Kim said inanely.

John glared venomously at her.—Well, thir nae fuckin good cauld! Yir Ma's gone tae a loat ay trouble tae make this meal, Kim! Show some appreciation! Like ah sais, some appreciation!

This was really worrying, as John seldom gave Kim a hard time; she was after all, his favourite. Kim pouted and lowered her head. She looked as if she was contemplating doing what she often did to get attention and bursting into tears, but had decided against it and was struggling to consider what other action she could take.

Vet got in on the act. She turned to Tony and snapped:—Tony, take yir fucking time. You n aw, Roy. That food isnae gaunna jump up 'n' run away bi' christ.

I had always thought of my Ma as young and beautiful. Now she seemed to me to look like a twisted, haggard old witch, staring out at me from behind a smudged mask of eyeliner. I noted the strands of silver in her long black hair.

She and the rest of them could fuck off. Ah wis going to be strong. Strong Strang. Ah wis gaunna make sure every cunt kent ma fuckin name.

Ah wis gaun . . .

DEEPER

DEEPER into the Marabou Stork nightmares.

Irvine Welsh (b. 1958)
Marabou Stork Nightmares, Cape (1995)

181

Brian Whittingham

Romance
and the Scottish Palate

Brought up;

on a diet of bridie chips bean
      with brown sauce and buttered bread
on a diet of square sausage bacon runny yolk eggs
      with fried bread and tottie scones
on a diet of steak pie black pudding battered hamburger
      with plenty of salt and vinegar
on a diet of minced beef n' dumplings
      with puff pastry squares
on a diet of a nice piece of Brisket
      with roast totties . . . on Sundays only

washed down with mugs
of tarry tea
and bottles of Irn Bru

cooked by his wife they parted

and he met a woman
who introduced him to the responsibility
of cooking for himself.

Sunflower seed vegetable bake —
lentil loaf—baked courgettes and broccoli spears
asparagus tips—crushed garlic and stuffed cabbage
      leaves
chick peas—hummous
and wild rice bake with red cabbage and peppers
kiwi-fruit and avocados

washed down with
a glass of Aqua-Libre or
a cup of coffee from her cafetière

they should have realised
their new recipe
was one they would never develop
a taste for.

Brian Whittingham
(written for this book)

Postcard from Jura

made soup today —
fried the onions in oil
added lentils and stirred
them around a bit
let them sweat
sliced carrot with your Japanese
cut-throat
and added that
then water, seasoning, herbs
and the veggie stock cube
you gave me last thing —
all brought to the boil
and simmered —
your recipe but lacking
the essential ingredient

Hamish Whyte (b. 1947)
A Sort of Hot Scotland, ASLS (1994)

Haggises

(from *Noctes* 26: June 1826)

SHEPHERD. . . . Tell me about the Haggis-Feast.

TICKLER A dozen of us entered our Haggises for a sweepstakes—and the match was decided at worthy Mrs Fergusson's, High Street. My haggis (they were all made, either by our wives or cooks, at our respective places of abode) ran second to Meg Dods's. The Director General's (which was what sporting men would have called a roarer) came in third—none of the others were placed.

SHEPHERD Did ony accident happen among the Haggises? I see by your face that ane at least among the dizzen played the deevil. I recollec' ance the awfu'est scene wi' a Haggis, in auld Mr Laidlaw's house. It was a great muckle big ane, answering to Robert Burns's description, wi' its hurdies like twa distant hills, and occupied the centre o' the table, round whilk sat about a score o' lads and lasses. The auld man had shut his een to ask a blessing, when some evil speerit put in into my head to gie the bag a slit wi' my gulley. Like water on the breakin' o' a dam, out rushed, in an instantawneous overflow, the inside o' the great chieftain o' the Pudding race, and the women-folk brak out into sic a shriek, that the master thocht somebody had drapped down dead. Meanwhile, its contents didna stop at the edge o' the table, but gaed ower wi' a sclutter upon the lads' breeks and the lassies' petticoats, burnin' the wearers to the bane; for what's hetter than a haggis?

TICKLER Nothing on this side of the grave.

SHEPHERD What a skirlin'! And then a' the colleys began yelpin' and youffin', for some o' them had their tauted hips scalded, and ithers o' them could na see for the stew that was rinnin' down their chafts. Glee'd Shooshy Dagleish fell a' her length in the thickest part o the inundation, wi' lang Tommy Potts aboon her, and we thocht they would never hae foun' their feet again, for the floor was as sliddery as ice—and—

NORTH Now, James, were you to write that down, and give it to the world in a book, it would be called coarse.

SHEPHERD Nae doubt. Everything nat'ral, and easy, and true, is ca'd coorse.

John Wilson (1785-1854)
Noctes Ambrosianae in *The Tavern Sages*
ed. J. H. Alexander, ASLS (1992)

'The Shepherd' and 'Christopher North' are fictionalised versions of James Hogg and John Wilson and 'Tickler' is based on Wilson's uncle Robert Sym. The *Noctes Ambrosianae* are a series of imaginary conversations set in William Ambrose's Edinburgh tavern.

Tenui musam meditamur avena.
We cultivate literature on a little oatmeal.

Sydney Smith (1771-1845)
Proposed motto for the *Edinburgh Review*

---

further reading

Brown, Catherine *Broths to Bannocks: Cooking in Scotland 1690 to the Present Day* John Murray, 1990
Brown, Catherine *Scottish Regional Recipes* Molendinar Press, 1981
Graham, Henry G *Social life of Scotland in the 18th Century* 2 vols 1899
Hope, Annette *A Caledonian Feast* Mainstream 1987
Lochhead, Marion *The Scots Household in the 18th Century* Moray Press 1948
MacClure, Victor *Scotland's Inner Man* Routledge 1935
McNeill, F. Marian *The Scots Kitchen: its lore and recipes* Blackie 1929; 2nd edition 1963
Plant, Marjorie *The Domestic Life of Scotland in the 18th Century* Edinburgh University Press 1952
Rogers, Charles *Social Life in Scotland from Early to Recent Times* 1884-86
Smout, T.C. *A History of the Scottish People 1560-1830* Collins 1972
Smout, T.C. *A Century of the Scottish People 1830-1950* Collins 1986
Steven, Maisie *The Good Scots Diet* Aberdeen University Press 1985
Tannahill, Reay *Food in History* Paladin 1975
Warrack, J. *Domestic Life in Scotland 1488-1688* 1920
Wilson, C. Anne *Food and Drink in Britain* Constable 1973

GENERAL INDEX

index

Scottish PEN

International PEN was founded in 1921 in the conviction that writers, given the freedom to transmit their thoughts within each nation and between nations, have much to contribute to international understanding and goodwill. The importance of PEN is as an international organisation linking writers from almost every country in the world. There are more than 120 centres throughout the world and PEN is recognised by UNESCO as a worldwide forum for writers.

The Scottish Centre of PEN, established in 1927 owes its existence to the initiative of High MacDiarmid. Over the years it has included amongst its members most of Scotland's best-known writers. Scottish PEN has currently around 200 members and invites applications from anyone who earns an income from writing and who subscribes to the aims of the organisation as enshrined in the PEN charter.

Please write to the Honorary Secretary, Scottish PEN, 33 Drumsheugh Gardens, Edinburgh EH3 7RN.

The International PEN Congress is held every year in a different country. The 1997 Congress will take place in Edinburgh and Glasgow in August. This is the first time in nearly fifty years that Scotland has hosted this prestigious event which draws in delegates and other writers from more than a hundred countries to discuss international issues, take part in a range of literary events and to make new friends and contacts.

Scottish PEN will host the main meeting of delegates which will discuss issues relating to freedom of speech and expression. A programme of events, exhibitions and performances is planned, some arranged jointly with the Edinburgh Book Festival.

Sales of *A Scottish Feast* are part of the fund-raising effort for the 1997 Congress.